Out for Blood

The Third of Severn

J. L. O'Rourke

Copyright 2018
Published by Millwheel Press Limited

ISBN Softcover 978-0-473-43989-7
Epub 978-0-473-43990-3
Kindle 978-0-473-43991-0

Discover other titles by J. L. O'Rourke
Blood in the Wings: The First of Severn
Chains of Blood: The Second of Severn
Power Ride: An Avi Livingstone murder mystery
Deep in the Shallows: A Lake Waihola Mystery
www.millwheelpress.co.nz

Acknowledgements:
While the majority of the characters in the Severn series are fictional inventions of my imagination and are not based on any real person, my thanks to the two real theatre crew who gave their permission to allow me to exaggerate their personalities and reinvent them into vampires, which have now developed their own truly fictional personalities. Those people know who they are – thank you. If anyone else thinks that they recognise themselves in a character – I guarantee that it is purely unintentional. Thanks, too, to my cover models, Skip and Michael.
Cover photo by Bethany Nehoff.

CHAPTER ONE

"I don't make the same mistake twice. I didn't kill her. Nothing is coming back to bite us."

"But you bit her, Aiden? Didn't you? After we left."

"Well, yes, of course I did. And, yes, I may have drunk a bit more than I should have but I guarantee you her heart was still beating when I took off."

Severn stood up, leant across the table and slammed the newspaper down in front of Aiden, who glared back, arms folded in defiance.

"So how did she wind up dead on New Brighton beach," Severn shouted, tapping the bold newspaper headline for emphasis.

"I don't know," Aiden shouted back, standing and leaning forwards until his forehead almost touched Severn's. "Maybe you went back for her. Or maybe he did." Aiden glared sideways at the smaller man seated between them. "Or maybe she just got on her bicycle and biked there. I repeat. I. Don't. Know!"

"Stop it, both of you!" I reached out my hand and waved it between their faces to get their attention. "Sit down. This is not helping. Maybe it's not even her." I picked up the paper and scanned the article. "It only says a woman's body has been found on New Brighton beach. It doesn't say it's Sally Murchison."

"That's true," the Reverend agreed. "Aiden, Severn, do as Riley says. Sit down and stop arguing. Just because Aiden has a bad habit of leaving bodies on beaches named Brighton, doesn't make him guilty of all of them. Anyway, to be fair, in the other cases Aiden was usually covering up for his sister."

"Other cases, plural?" I chimed in. "I know about the one a few months ago, last time you guys were here, but are you saying there were more?"

"Well," the Reverend rubbed his long fingers over his chin in an attempt to look nonchalant, "there was that one in Dunedin forty years ago that Severn got mixed up in, although that was closer to Taieri Mouth than Brighton but I guess that's splitting hairs, and there may have been one or two incidents in England's Brighton but they were well spread out. It's been at least seventy years since the last one. Anyway, back to today's little revelation. Yes, we know we left Aiden with her when we rescued that ghastly child, Tommy. Yes, we did leave Aiden with instructions to sort her out. Yes, we know Aiden can get a bit … um … enthusiastic but I, for one, trust him and if he says she was alive when he left, I am going to believe him. I would suggest for now that we let this go and get on with the show. We have a matinee in two hours. Let's just get to Mona Vale, get the gear rigged and worry about this when we find out who the woman is. If the police confirm it's Sally Murchison, we can panic then."

I could see by the way his eyes narrowed behind his glasses that Severn did not agree but the tiny Reverend David Rochester was the boss and, even though the other two towered over him, they did as he ordered. But I wasn't one of them, yet, and the Rev didn't scare me. I grabbed my boyfriend by the arm.

"Yeah, grab your stuff, Sev. We have to get Grant's car back to him. They will be nearly ready to go too. Did I leave my torch in your room?"

I didn't give him a chance to answer my purposefully stupid question, I just hoped he would follow me into the motel bedroom he had claimed as his, which he did, a bemused expression on his face. Before he could say anything I put a finger to my lips as a sign to be quiet then both fingers to my ears followed by an index finger pointing to the room we had just left. He got the message. I had something to say but I didn't want the others to hear it, which meant wait until we were a few blocks away in the car, well out of vampire hearing range. With a quick nod of his head, Severn picked up his long, black coat and motioned for us to leave.

"See you guys at the show," I called out as cheerfully as I could fake while we bolted out of the motel. Severn drove four blocks before he asked me what I wanted to say.

"Well," I hesitated, "The Rev may trust Aiden but I'm not entirely sure I trust the Rev."

"What? Why?"

"Thinking back. It's Sunday now. We rescued Tommy from Sally Murchison on Friday night. I know we were all at the show yesterday but Aiden and the Rev were late. You were covering for them, saying that they were sleeping, but you walked to my place yesterday. If they had been at the motel sleeping, the car would have been there and you would have driven. I challenged you on that and you admitted that you only walked because they had gone out somewhere in the car, been out all night, hadn't come back, and you had no idea where they were or what they were doing. Right?"

Severn nodded.

"Plus," I continued, "when I asked Aiden what happened to Sally, had he paid her off like he was told to do, he just said she was gone. He said yes she's gone and she won't be back. When I asked him how he could be so sure, he said, and I quote, after he had finished with her, she would not be back. I asked what he had done to her and he said it was nothing I needed to worry about, he had just done what he was told to do. What he was good at. So what is it he is good at? From what I just heard, he is good at leaving bodies on Brighton beaches."

Severn fixed his eyes on the road so I couldn't see his expression. "Maybe the Rev is being completely truthful," he said. "He told us he believed Aiden didn't kill Sally. But what if he's not telling the whole story?"

"What?"

"Think about it. They were together. Sally died. Aiden didn't kill her. Who does that leave?"

I looked at Severn in horror. He looked away from the road long enough to nod his head and flash me a weak smile.

"The Reverend."

CHAPTER TWO

For backstage crew, Severn and I were good actors, pretending we had nothing to worry about, smiling happily as we pulled into our driveway to collect Mum and my stepfather, Grant, and laughing at Grant's weak jokes on the drive to Mona Vale. Severn even managed such a cheerful greeting for Cameron, the spunky boy-racer followspot operator, that nobody would have known how jealous they were of each other. Imagine that – plain, ordinary, boring Riley Lowe having two sexy guys competing for her. What a pity Tasha Moreland of the upthrust bra wasn't around – that would have driven her nuts.

Sunday matinees are always a hard slog. The audience is always a mix of old people and family groups with young children, so the energy level is always low, and the crew and actors are all exhausted and a bit hung-over from the obligatory Saturday night after-show party so their energy level is non-existent. I didn't envy the stage manager who had to rev everybody up to put on a decent performance. Especially as the stage was set on a large lawn with no shelter and the temperature was climbing before the show even started.

I had my usual argument with the musicians about the level of their instruments, which I won, as always, by nodding my head as if I was agreeing with them, twiddling the knobs and faders on the sound desk, then resetting them exactly as they had been at the beginning. Severn had his own dramas, deftly saving our desk from the hands of an audience member who thought he knew more about sound desks than we did. He was just about to start pulling out plugs when Severn appeared beside him, sliding between the man and the sound desk so they were so close the man's breath was steaming up Severn's glasses. Quietly but with menacing politeness, Severn threatened the man with bodily harm if he touched a single cable. The guy laughed as if Severn had cracked the funniest joke. Severn didn't move. I guess the guy thought Severn looked young, inexperienced and in need of expert advice, as he started blustering about what experience he had and where the cables should be plugged but a hissed command to

"Sit...Down...Sir" made him realise his mistake. With a mumbled comment about young upstarts, he submitted, climbed down off the scaffolding and scurried away to join his family on the grass.

Cameron wasn't faring any better. One bank of parcan lights, the one at the very top of a tall scaffolding tower, wasn't working. The head lighting guy, Danny, was checking the cables, running along the ground while Cameron was scampering up and down the scaffolding like a demented monkey. I noticed that Aiden and the Reverend were helping them – staying well out of the way of Severn and me. That was fine by us – we didn't feel like talking to them until we had figured a few things out. Between the two of us, without their help, we laid out and connected the seemingly endless lengths of speaker cable, fitted batteries to the radio microphones, and checked them all.

I left Severn guarding the desk in case our helpful punter came back, and raced around the back of the stage to the dressing room tents, set up on a smaller lawn on the other side of a tiny creek. In the men's dressing room I was subjected to the usual rubbish talk as I tucked microphone packs into men's pants and taped the tiny wires up their bare backs and over their ears to their cheeks. Tommy, the brat child, stood quietly while I fixed his mic – too scared of me to object. In the women's tent the talk was all about gardening and what colour decorations somebody's daughter was having at their wedding. Nobody mentioned the body on the beach, not even Heidi McCormack, Tommy's mother, so maybe it wasn't Sally. Unless it was, and Heidi didn't know yet.

With a quick wave to Mum who was braiding the hair of one of the chorus members, I raced back to my seat behind the sound desk. Severn was already in place and handed me my comms headphones as I slid into the chair beside him. As I heard the stage manager call "five minutes to beginners" through my comms, I heard Severn speaking quietly beside me but not into any microphone.

"Aiden, David, where are you? Aiden, I need you backstage looking after the radio mics. Reverend, you're on standby to troubleshoot. But I need to know where you are."

Even though I was sitting beside him, I could barely make out his quiet voice but I knew, with their incredible hearing, the vampires would hear every word. I didn't hear their reply but by the grim tightening of his mouth and eyes, I gathered Severn wasn't impressed and it probably wasn't polite. Just as I was about to ask, a smiling Aiden joined us in the scaffolding tower.

"Don't get your knickers in a knot," he said. "We're all good to go." He turned to climb out of the tower then stopped. Holding on by one hand, he swung backwards from one of the bars until his face was at Severn's shoulder. "And get out of this mood the two of you are in. Rev and I know what you're thinking and you're wrong. I'll prove it to you later."

Then he jumped. We were so high up the tower I almost expected to see him unfurl his wings and fly, which was impossible as he was fully dressed in his stage blacks. Instead he landed in a dive roll, picked himself up and lifted his hand to his head in a salute that turned into a single finger gesture that told us exactly what he thought of us. Severn muttered a curse under his breath that we both knew Aiden would hear. I gave him one of the fake "I'm so happy today" smiles I had been pretending since we left the motel. He growled back. I pulled a bar of chocolate from my pocket, took a bite and settled at the desk, my hands hovering over the sliders. Over the comms the stage manager called "standby" and I forgot about Sally Murchison. The show had begun.

The actors suffered in the heat of a summer Sunday afternoon, melting in their velvet costumes, but the audience didn't seem to notice or care. I had a script in front of me so I knew when the guy playing Robin Hood forgot his lines and jumped into another scene, leaving Friar Tuck to pull the dialogue back to the scene they were actually in, and when Maid Marion called Robin Hood by his proper name, but the audience cheered the Merry Men, booed the Sheriff and his troops and applauded with wolf whistles as the actors came on stage for the curtain call.

The vampires suffered more. Matinees were their worst nightmare. It wasn't that they couldn't go out in the sunshine – they didn't really turn to dust – but it left them sick and lethargic. Aiden and the Reverend spent most of the show sitting in the crawlspace under the stage but Severn was stuck beside me in the tower. The tarpaulin rigged over our desk and chairs provided a bit of shade but I could tell Severn was struggling as the sun rose higher. I wanted to tell him to keep hydrated but I wasn't sure if that made any difference to vampires, so it was a huge relief when we heard the stage manager remind us all that our next show was on Wednesday, and sign off – our call to start dismantling the gear and stacking it away.

Mum and Grant caught up with me as I was coiling the last few cables. Mum held out a bar of chocolate, which I snatched and stuffed into my mouth. Mum laughed.

"Do you and Severn need a ride with us or are you going with the others?" she asked. "Or the lighting boy?" she added in a tone that was far too innocent.

"Stop stirring, Mum! Just go home, you two. I'm going with Severn. We have things to do. He can drop me home later."

As they walked away I gathered up the cables and took them to the storage container where I found Aiden, the Reverend and Cameron packing away the lighting and sound equipment. Severn sat to one side under the shade of a tree, his head in his hands.

"Are you okay?" I asked, sitting beside him on the grass. "Was the sun that bad?"

"I reckon he's got heat stroke," Cameron called out. "He looks like shit."

"He always looks like that," Aiden joked from inside the container.

"Smart arse," Severn muttered. "But, yes, it was just too hot up there on the tower. I need to get back to the motel and sit in the dark."

"If you're waiting for these two, Danny and I can finish here and you guys can all go," Cameron offered. "Go on, get out of here and I'll see you Wednesday."

The drive back to the motel was quiet. Severn lay on the back seat, his head on my lap. I could tell Aiden wanted to say something as he kept looking at me in the rear view mirror, then changing his mind and staring at the road as if he had forgotten the way. When we reached the motel Aiden slammed the car door and walked ahead of us, leaving the Reverend to help Severn out of the car and into his room. I dumped Severn's coat on the floor, made sure the curtains were drawn to keep out the light and left Severn to recover. I wasn't sure what that would entail but I had a horrible feeling it would include going out later on a feeding expedition. I didn't want to think about the details.

I settled for making myself a coffee in their tiny kitchen so I could talk to the Reverend.

"We need to find out more about that body on the beach," I started.

"Why?"

"Because I want to know if it was Sally Murchison."

"Why? What does it matter if it was or wasn't her?"

"Really? You can't figure that out? If it's Sally then the McCormacks are going to find out. Even if the police never make a connection with Tommy's kidnapping, the McCormacks will. Then they will start asking dear little Tommy difficult questions and he will tell them about us. About you. About Severn flying him down the hill from Sally's house."

"And who is going to believe him?"

"It's not about believing him. It's about the police asking any questions at all. You know Severn can't afford to be questioned by the police. Even though they know he didn't kill Tasha, there is still the fact of his fingerprints from that body forty years ago. That one cop remembered him. I don't really care if Aiden killed Sally – well I do care but I am past thinking about it – I am just hoping that he wasn't stupid enough to dump her on New Brighton beach. I need to know who that body was."

"I need to know that too." Aiden came out of his bedroom and flung himself onto the couch beside the Reverend. "Like I told you earlier, I can guarantee that it isn't Mad Sally. I'm much tidier than that. They won't find her for years." I glared at him, repulsed by all the information included in what he hadn't said. He grinned at me. "I did my job. She was alive when I left her, like I said, but okay, I may have gone back later. I cleaned up. Don't ask."

"So it's entirely coincidental that a woman has turned up dead the day after you 'cleaned up' Sally?" I was still sceptical.

"Of course it is," Aiden bit back. "People die all the time. It's probably some swimmer. Or someone who jumped off the pier."

"Well, I'm going to find out," I said. "There's no point me sitting around here – Sev needs to sleep and I'm guessing you will all be going out for your usual take-away meals later – and I am not having any part of that – so I'm going home." I held out my hand as Aiden started to rise from the couch. "No, stay there. I can walk. See you later."

I stepped back out into the searing heat of the bright sunshine, thinking as I walked. Something about the body on the beach had Aiden worried so, if it wasn't Sally, what was he scared of? I was so engrossed in my thoughts I hardly noticed the shadow.

CHAPTER THREE

Mum's expression turned from surprise to concern when she saw me walk in the door.

"What are you doing home? Are you all right? Have you and Severn had an argument?"

"No, no, we're fine. Well, I'm fine but Sev isn't feeling well. He got heat stroke out in the sun today, so he's lying down in the dark for a while."

"Hmm, yes, I wondered how they would cope with an outdoor matinee. Still, by now I guess they've learned their tolerance levels. They cope better than I would have expected them to."

"What?" She knew. My mother was always making little digs and jokes that suggested she knew the boys were vampires but she had never been this open about it. Where was this conversation heading? Did I want to have this conversation at all? Ever?

"Tolerance. Of the sun. Vampires. I didn't think they could stay out in the sun."

"Vampires? How did we get onto vampires. What are you talking about, Mum?"

Mum laughed, put down the magazine she was holding and patted the couch seat beside where she was sitting. "You said it the other day when we were shopping. I commented on how the boys look so young but seem so knowledgeable and sure of themselves, and you said it was because they were vampires. So you started it. I was just agreeing with you. Sun, vampires, not a good mix."

"No." I decided to play along but stayed standing so I could end the conversation and escape as soon as possible. "Bad mix. It was okay for Aiden and the Rev because they were under the stage most of the time but Sev's really sick now. He'll be okay though. He didn't turn to dust and disappear."

"Just as well. What do you take a sick vampire? Chicken soup or chicken blood?"

"Really, Mother! Enough!"

"At least they won't get sunburnt. Not like you. Your nose looks like Rudolph the Reindeer."

"Gee, thanks."

"You're welcome. Anyway, seeing as you're here, and not there with them, what do you say about going to the beach for tea? I can't be bothered cooking but we need to eat. Grant and I were going to buy fish and chips and eat them down at the beach. Do you want to join us or are you planning on going back to the motel?"

The beach. Oh, great! Let's walk along the beach where the body was found and talk about vampires. Awesome!

"Yep, sounds good to me. Just give me time to get changed." Without waiting for a reply, I disappeared into my bedroom and closed the door. I needed time to think.

I hoped Mum would pick Sumner beach, not New Brighton, but we did go to New Brighton and it didn't do my head in as I had worried it would. Grant parked the car in a quiet spot away from the crowds of normal non-theatre people who were taking advantage of the warm summer evening to do normal non-theatre things like swimming and making sand castles. We pretended to be normal too, taking off our shoes to walk barefoot along the hot sand. We even looked normal - Grant in his khaki cargo shorts and green polo shirt, Mum in a floaty, floral summer dress, and me in a short, denim skirt and a white t-shirt sporting a series of letters that looked enigmatic but meant absolutely nothing. Nice normal attire for the beach.

Mum had brought a rug which she spread out on the sand, Grant unfolded the parcel of fish and chips and we sat, enjoying the tranquility. The best thing about Sunday matinees was not having to race back for an evening performance. We were on our own time.

"What's that down there?" Mum asked, pointing with a chip at a piece of yellow that flapped from the end of a hunk of driftwood further down the beach.

I had a horrible feeling I knew exactly what it was and I didn't want anything to do with it. I shrugged my shoulders and gave an unintelligible grunt that I hoped would put an end to her speculation but, as I expected, that wasn't enough for Mum. She lowered her head and raised her eyebrows in a look that I swear she had stolen from Severn's repertoire of wordless head movements that told you exactly what he was thinking. I gave in and went to look.

There was nothing to be gained from going to where the woman's body had been lying but once I reached the spot, something drew me closer. I couldn't explain why but I had to stand there, right on the high tide mark, where she was. There were no marks on the sand, no sign left of where they had found her, just one remnant of crime scene tape still tied to the driftwood, the rest of it blown away in the nor'west wind. If it was Sally, she left no memorial. The spot on the sand was identical to the rest of the beach. What had I expected? For no reason I could explain, I scuffed my feet through the sand, creating meaningless swirls, then walked back to flop down onto the rug.

"Crime scene tape," I said. "That must have been where they found that woman."

"What woman?" Grant asked.

"The one in the paper. The one in the news." Was Grant kidding? They didn't know?

"Oh, I must have missed that. What happened?"

"I don't know," I answered truthfully. "Severn and I saw the headline when we went to the dairy for milk this morning. Some woman's body found on the beach. That bit of yellow is tape so I'm guessing that's where she was."

"Oh, that's sad," Mum said. "That's the trouble when we're neck-deep in a show – we miss all the stuff happening in the real world." She turned to me and narrowed her eyes in a tiny, slightly evil smile. "Not bitten by vampires and drained of blood, I hope?"

"In your dreams." I emphasised my reply by sticking out my tongue at her.

Fortunately, Mum kept any more vampire comments to herself and Grant remained oblivious to the sub-text of the exchange. I changed the subject with an inane comment about the wind getting chilly, which wasn't true, adding a pretend shiver which had the desired effect. Grant agreed the wind was changing, suggested we head home and made the first move to stand up. Mum automatically followed with the rug. I looked back at the flapping yellow of the crime scene tape and decided I had to find out more. What if it really was Sally?

Back at home I couldn't settle. I turned on my computer and searched all the news sites but there was nothing new on the beach woman. All the stories said the same thing – that a body had been found. Nothing else. No description, no guess at her age, no hair colour, no other information. No help at all.

I thought about going around to the motel to check on Severn, discarded the idea then picked it up again. If Severn was still sick, he would be asleep. He wouldn't want to see me but I wouldn't wake him. I would just ask the Rev how he was and leave. If he was okay then they would be planning their night's feeding and I didn't want to get involved with that but it wouldn't be dark enough for hunting for a few more hours and they wouldn't discuss it in front of me. Well, Severn and the Rev wouldn't. Either way I had nothing better to do and I couldn't sit still.

A few minutes later I was collecting my bike from the garage but as I was pedalling out of our drive a movement caught my eye. I glanced sideways but where I had thought I had seen a figure, there was only the neighbour's tree. I turned my head back to concentrate on the road and again thought I caught a glimpse of movement, this time from the other side of the street. Without turning my head, and looking obvious, I stole a glance at my bike's rear-view mirror. I was sure I saw a shadow slip behind the neighbour's house. Aiden?

I couldn't prove it, but I was sure the shadow followed me to the motel. I never saw an actual figure but whenever I stopped at a corner or glanced in my mirror I saw flashes. I caught another glimpse of the shadow as I reached the motel and leant my bike against its wall. Something dark flitted across the driveway and disappeared behind the unit at the far end of the motel block. If I had been a bit creeped out by it as I was cycling, now I was just plain angry. What the hell was going on? Why was I being followed? If Aiden had anything to say, why didn't he just say it to my face? Did he still think I was having it off with Cameron behind Severn's back? Was he following me to find out? This B-grade spy stuff was ridiculous and it was starting to piss me off in a big way. Ready to tell the Reverend what I thought of his friend's childish behaviour, I barged through the door without knocking. Aiden and the Rev were both sitting on the couch, mouth's hanging open at my furious entrance.

"What's up?" the Rev asked.

"How did you get in here so fast?" I pointed at Aiden.

"What do you mean, fast?" Aiden asked. "I've been here since you left earlier. I haven't done anything fast for hours."

"Then what followed me? Severn? Is he up?"

"No. He hasn't moved. Why?"

"Because something or someone followed me from my place

and I thought it was you. But it obviously wasn't, because you're here."

"What did they look like?" the Reverend asked.

"I don't know. I never actually saw them. Just a shape that kept disappearing every time I looked at it directly. That's why I assumed it was you, Aiden. You guys are the only ones who can move that fast and that stealthily."

The Reverend moved to look out the window, turned back and shook his head.

"I can't see anything out there now. Look, we're all still a bit jumpy after the Tommy kidnapping, maybe it was just the wind blowing things around. Or the light reflecting off windows, or cars."

"Yeah, maybe." I sat down on the nearest chair and rested my head in my hands. He was talking rubbish and we all knew it but I couldn't find the energy to argue. Through my fingers I saw Aiden's lips move. I couldn't hear anything so I knew he was whispering, just loud enough that the Reverend would hear him. Aiden raised an eyebrow. I rocked my head back, pulling my hands down my face as if I was tired, but really so I could move my head so I could see the Rev. He was whispering back to Aiden. They knew something that they weren't telling me. I'd had enough. I had to leave.

Outside, I checked the time on my watch. Not quite seven o'clock. Still early. I didn't want to go home but where could I go? I reached for my phone and sent my best friend, Anita, a text asking if she wanted a visitor. It only took a few seconds for her reply to pop up and I was back on my bike, pedalling fast. I thought I saw the shadow as I left the motel but it didn't follow me. Or I didn't see it.

CHAPTER 4

Anita was exactly where I expected her to be – tucked up cross-legged on her bed cuddling a fluffy toy bunny. What I didn't expect was Caleb - violin player, chemistry nerd and father of Anita's unborn baby – perched on the bed beside her, also clutching a toy rabbit.

"You've been brainwashed," I said to him as I pulled the pink, metal office chair from its neat position under her immaculately tidy, white corner desk and subsided into it. "The rabbit," I continued as he looked completely confused. "She's got you cuddling her rabbits already. There is no hope now. You are heading down the slippery slope into Anitaworld. You have been warned."

Caleb looked down at the toy and shook his head as if he had just noticed he was holding it. A blush started in his ears then spread across his face which made me feel bad as I hadn't intended to embarrass him. With a weak smile, he placed the toy carefully on the bed with all the others that covered it, and pulled himself upright.

"I'll let you guys catch up," he said. "Call me later."

The blush had crept around his neck to mingle with his red curls. I could see he wanted to give Anita a goodbye kiss but embarrassment won and, with a mumbled "goodbye", he scurried out the door. Anita threw her toy rabbit at me.

"You're so mean. Don't tease him like that."

"Sorry. Didn't mean to be mean. I just didn't expect him to be here. He blushes easily. Do you think your baby will be a ginger?" I pronounced ginger with a hard g so it rhymed with bringer.

"Probably. An absolute carrot top. With curls. Anyway, what's the goss? Come on, out with it, fill me in."

"You first. I gather that you and Caleb are getting on? Are you actually a couple now? As opposed to him just being the guy who got you drunk and got you pregnant."

"A couple? Yeah, I guess we are. Once everybody calmed down and our dads stopped yelling at each other, Caleb and I decided to sit down and talk. And guess what? We actually like each other.

We've discovered we've got heaps of things in common. I mean, we're both into music. He's way better than I am – he's been accepted into the Youth Orchestra with his violin and I'm only grade four on my flute – but at least I understand what he's talking about. I know an arpeggio from an andante."

"That's a good start."

"Yes. And good incentive to practise more and sit my grade five exam. But wait, there's more. Even though he's a science geek and I suck at it, it turns out we're both into medieval history. His parents are science fiction fans so they are into the whole role-playing stuff. Caleb's been brought up going to MFR events and he's going to take me along to the next one. They sound like fun."

"MFR? What's that?"

"The Medieval and Fantasy Recreationists. Everybody creates a persona for themselves and dresses up in medieval costumes. Apparently there's lots of music and sword play – and feasting, lots of feasting."

"Your persona will have to be some crazy forest rabbit whisperer. I know, attach a whole lot of toy rabbits to the back of your dress and walk along playing your flute, like the Pied Piper."

"Nooo! That's just weird. I'm going to be glamourous. Pregnant but glamourous. Caleb's mum is going to help me make my costume. She's got heaps of patterns."

"Well, I'm glad to hear you two are getting on. It's going to be tough just being pregnant. It would be a lot harder if you and Caleb hated each other."

"Yeah. I expected him to walk away and want nothing to do with me or the baby but he's really stepped up. He's actually looking forward to it."

"Now I feel mean for not being nicer to him last year. He was always a bit of an outcast. Maybe we should've included him a bit more."

"Yeah. But you know what? He knows he's on the outside and he doesn't care. I think he kind of likes it there. He's way more used to being with adults and I don't think he fits in very well with people his own age. I can understand it though. He was home schooled all through primary school. He only enrolled at Eastgate last year so he could sit his NCEA so he can get into university. He's going to do a double degree in music and chemistry."

"So he's not going to be earning a living until the baby's in high school?"

"Maybe not. But I am. Starting next month."

"What?" I gasped. "You're pregnant. What are you going to do?"

"Train and earn at the same time. I've found a place where I can study to be a preschool teacher and work at a preschool while I train. It'll be perfect because once baby arrives he, she, whatever, can come to work with me. All sorted."

"Well, knock me down with a toy rabbit. You are so organised. What have you done with Anita?"

"Ha ha. But enough of me. What have you been up to? How are you and Severn? It must have been so amazing when he came back. I got your text and I've been imagining it – you, sitting behind your desk thingy and looking up, Severn appearing like something from a movie. It's just so romantic."

"Romantic wasn't my first reaction," I laughed. "Okay, it was the second, and maybe the third, but first it was just sheer relief. I was so overwhelmed. I still can't believe that the Mad Hatters expected me to run their whole sound department. With no help. I have never been so pleased to see those three."

"Three?"

"Yeah, two of the other crew members came too. The ones I told you about. The little, short guy that everyone calls the Reverend even though his name's David, and Aiden, who I didn't have much to do with last time. He's got a weird sense of humour and can be a bit creepy when he's trying to be funny but, like Sev and the Rev, he knows what he's doing backstage. They've been helping the lighting guys too, so we're all really glad they tagged along."

"How long is he staying? Does he have to go straight back to France?"

"I don't know," I said. "The show has only just opened so he'll stay till it closes. I'm hoping he might stay on a bit longer after that, but I don't know yet."

"Am I detecting some hesitancy?" Anita asked, snuggling her bunny tighter. "Relief instead of romance and now you're not sure whether he's staying or going? What are you not telling me? Are you two okay?"

"To be honest? I don't know." I let out a long breath between clenched teeth, something between a sigh and a whistle, and swapped seats to join Anita on the bed. Automatically, she handed me the toy rabbit Caleb had been cuddling and, just as automatically, I held it tight as I pulled my thoughts together.

"It's the other guy, isn't it?" Anita jumped in before I had a chance to speak. "The one with the car. You're a friggin' idiot!" I drew breath to answer but Anita continued. "Seriously? What is wrong with you? You score an amazing boyfriend who A", she raised her right index finger to her outstretched left hand so she could tick off her points one at a time, "spends his life in theatres, exactly the same as you. B," she ticked another finger, "hangs around with a group who can teach you all the backstage stuff you want to learn to do. C," a third finger, "obviously, from what you've said, isn't too shabby looking and D," the fourth finger, "flew half way around the world in his own private plane to help you when you were stuck. His own private plane! So, as well as caring about you, he's obviously got money to burn."

"It's not his plane," I objected. "It belongs to the company."

"Don't split hairs! Could I click my fingers and summon up a plane? My point is, how can you possibly be looking sideways at some boy from the east side with a noisy car? Or am I missing something? Is Severn not the nice guy you thought he was? He's not violent or anything, is he?"

"No, no." I waved a hand to fend off the idea. "Not at all."

"But it's not all rosy?"

"Not quite," I admitted. "We had an argument the other day. Or rather, I got angry with him but it wasn't his fault. It was me getting things wrong. And today wasn't so great, but again, that wasn't really his fault. Some stuff came up and we're just seeing opposite sides of it." Yeah, the human side and the vampire side.

"And now you're not talking to him, which is why you're here, talking to me."

"No. Wrong again. I'm here talking to you because he's asleep. It was stinking hot at the matinee today and Sev got heat stroke. I left him sleeping it off. He was pretty sick."

"Oh, that sucks. I hope he's better by Wednesday. I'll finally get to meet your mystery man."

"Are you coming to the show?"

"Yes. Caleb and his parents are going so I'm tagging along. Apparently Caleb's dad taught the actors how to fight with staves for the scene on the bridge."

"Small world, eh? We'll be there an hour or so before you guys, so come and find me. I'll be somewhere around the big scaffolding tower."

"Which one's Severn? Will I know him when I see him."

"He'll be the one looking serious." I was about to add more when my phone pinged a message. I pulled it out of my pocket to check the screen. Severn.

> *R u ok? can we meet?*
> *with anita. meet you at edmonds gardens in 30 min*
> *sweet, c u soon*

"Severn?" Anta asked.

"Yep, gotta go."

"See you Wednesday."

Severn arrived like a true vampire and scared the hell out of me.

There was no sign of him when I pedalled up, so I locked my bike to a metal pole in the car park and walked through the gate into the small Bluebird garden at the back end of the Edmonds Gardens complex. The evening was darkening. Away from the streetlights and under the shelter of the towering trees, it was hard to see the path so I had my head down, looking at the ground in front of me, when I was grabbed.

An arm swept around my waist, pulling me backwards, a hand pushed against my ear, tilting my head to the side, the sharp edge of a tooth ran along my exposed neck. I screamed. He held me tighter, muttered something unintelligible but low and soothing and licked my neck. His breathing was ragged. So was mine. My heartbeat sped up and I know he felt it, heard it pulsing faster, as his breath quickened, rippling across my skin in waves. I leant back into his embrace, closed my eyes and tilted my head further to the side.

"Bite me."

Severn's hand smoothed my hair, holding it out of the way as his lips tasted my skin. His breath shuddered. I held mine. There was pressure, a sharp sting then absolute bliss. Like an earthquake, the reality was probably only a few seconds but it felt like forever. I was enthralled, jubilant, yet disappointed when it ended and Severn pulled away with a last lick to wipe away the drop of blood that trickled down my neck. I turned to face him, my body raging with desire. When I lifted my arms and pulled his head down to kiss him, I could taste my blood on his lips.

There was no need for words, we both knew what we wanted. Severn swung me into his arms and carried me deeper into the garden, turning down the manicured floral aisle to lay me on the green grass of the wedding altar. The sweet smell of roses mingled with the taste of my own blood then both were overtaken by the unique leathery scent of vampire. In a deft move, my underwear was gone and Severn was on top of me, in me, moving me against him. When I thought it was impossible to feel any more ecstatic, that I would burst, he bit me again.

As we lay on the grass, wrapped in each other, staring at the night sky, I realised the truth – no human male was ever going to be good enough. And I wasn't sure if being a human was good enough for me. If that was a glimpse into the heightened senses of the vampire world, I wanted more. I wanted to stay there.

CHAPTER FIVE

What do I wear? Mum is going to notice the bite marks.

I ended up sleeping by myself. I didn't want to go home but there was no alternative. Much as we wanted to stay together, Severn didn't want to take me back to the motel where he knew Aiden would spoil the mood with rude comments, and Severn staying in my room wasn't an option either – even though he had done it before. But it was different now. Very different. Reluctantly, I kissed him goodnight at the end of our driveway, wheeled my bike into the garage and crept inside, hoping that Mum had gone to bed.

It took me a long time to fall asleep. Thoughts, feelings, memories swirled in my brain, swept through my body, emotions fighting with reason. Human, vampire, lust, feeding, love, bloodlust – where were the boundaries? Were there any boundaries any more? Had I crossed over the last one? No, not the last one – I was still human.

I must have slept because it was daylight when I woke up. I lay for a while, enjoying the comfort of my warm bed, letting my thoughts wander back through last night. Eventually the sound of Mum's voice singing that infernally cheerful 'Good Morning' song from 'Singin' in the Rain' forced me into action. She was worse than an alarm clock. I knew the only way to shut her up was to appear, looking awake. Which brought me to the question of what to wear. It was going to be another hot day – no excuse at all for a high necked jersey and if I turned up in a scarf she would be immediately suspicious as that was so not my style. To gain time I yelled out that I was going to have a shower and dashed into the bathroom.

Not that I needed to worry. I rushed to the mirror, pulled back my hair and tilted my head to look at the bite marks. Talk about relief! I was expecting the classic B-grade movie fang prints on the side of my neck but Severn had bitten me further back, lower down, more on my shoulder than my neck. The marks were tiny, fine, just specks of red. I could pass them off as mosquito bites – if Mum even noticed them. When I let my long, blonde hair go, it cascaded over my shoulders, obliterating the spot completely. I laughed to myself. All through rehearsals in the hot sun I had been so sick of my hair – wishing I had time to get it cut. Now I was glad it had grown so long. It might be annoying but it was useful camouflage. I showered, dressed and went in search of strong coffee.

The singing alarm clock that was my mother had swapped from musicals to Motown. Diana Ross and the Supremes were blaring from the stereo and Mum was singing along, full blast, while she vacuumed the lounge carpet. I joined in a chorus. It's not right that someone my age knows all the lyrics of songs from way before I was born, but Mum played them all the time so there was no escape. I could sing them all before I could read or write.

To distract her from asking questions about me, I filled Mum in on the gossip about Anita and Caleb, including Anita's decision to train as a preschool teacher. Mum was suitably impressed.

"What about you?" she asked as she lifted an ornament to dust the shelf under it. "Have you decided what you're going to do? I fully understand why you're not doing year thirteen – you haven't exactly enjoyed the last few years at school – but you probably need to make a decision soon on what you do want to do. You'll be seventeen in a few weeks. Are you going to take your father up on his offer of a gap year in Australia?"

Yesterday my answer would have been "I don't know" but all of a sudden it was crystal clear.

"No. Sorry, Dad, it's no to Australia but yes, believe it or not, I have actually made a decision. Having the whole sound department dumped on me for this show has been terrifying, and there's no way I would have coped without Severn and the other guys. It's made me realise how little I know and how much I need to learn. So, if it's okay with you, I think I want to enrol in MAINZ and do their certificate in live sound engineering. If I'm going to spend the rest of my life backstage, I may as well know what I'm doing."

"The rest of your life, huh? You wouldn't be planning on touring with a professional crew by any chance? One that we might know?"

"Yeah ... well ... maybe." Hell yes, definitely. And if I make the final decision it could be a very long life.

Mum gave me one of her long, searching looks that make me sure she can read my mind then smiled.

"I'm sure with your experience, you'll have no trouble getting accepted onto the course. At least, if you travel off across the world with that lot, I know they will look after you. And maybe once a year you'll come back and work our show for free." She walked to the kitchen and put down her duster. "I see they've named that woman who was found on the beach. It's in the paper."

"Oh," I grabbed the paper off the table, "Who is she?" Please don't let it be Sally Murchison.

It wasn't.

"Oh my god! Mum, we know her. It's Julia."

"Who?"

"Julia, from our theatre company. She's crew. She was one of the assistant stage managers last year. You must remember her. Beth worked my side of the stage and Julia worked the other." I could see Mum's brain ticking over.

"Skinny, beanpole of a girl. I remember," Mum said. "She was always chatting up Seth, the gorgeous flyman with the muscles. Wasn't he Severn's boss – the head of the travelling crew?"

"Yeah, bossy being the operative word. Severn's pretty happy he doesn't have to deal with him any more."

"Has the crew split up? Is that why there are only three of them this time?"

I wasn't going to tell Mum that they had more than split up – Seth was well and truly dead, staked through the heart in true vampire fashion by Severn.

"Seth's gone off to do his own thing," I lied, "but the girls, Meredith and Olivia, are still around. They're both in France with Finn." Under guard by Finn to be more precise.

"They were an odd pair, those girls. Not very friendly. Anyway, that's a shame about Julia. I'll have to tell Grant. He will want to attend the funeral if she was one of our crew members."

I sat down at the table to read the newspaper article properly. Julia's body had been found by an early morning dog walker. The police were puzzled as there were no signs of how she got to where she was found. There were no footsteps in the sand and no convenient car or means of transport abandoned nearby. There were also no obvious signs of death. The reporter speculated that she must have walked along the beach below the high tide mark so her footprints had disappeared when the tide came in and the police hinted at death by natural causes but said they would know more after the autopsy. I knew they were missing something and Severn would be in big trouble when they found it.

This was going to get messy. When the police noticed similarities with the other body found on the beach a few months ago, which they were going to do soon if they hadn't already, they were going to start looking for Severn. Sure, last time, when Natasha was killed in the theatre and Severn was hunted for it, the vampires got him out of the country, but it was on a false passport, the same way he had come back in, so as far as the police were concerned, he never left. Which meant he was still here, which he was, which also meant they would start looking for him soon and the first place they would look would be the last place they saw him – backstage with us.

CHAPTER SIX

"Are you guys listening to me? Do you realise how serious this is?" I waved the newspaper in the Rev's face. "We need to figure out who's doing this."

"Calm down and breathe," the Rev said. "And sit down. You came in here like a crazy person. Slow down."

He was right, I had barged in like a crazy person. The whole thing had been buzzing around in my head for the past two hours, spinning, growing, spreading, twisting until I was tripping over myself mentally trying to sort out the ramifications. I had tried to find ordinary things to do at home, I had even sat on my bed and remembered all the things that had happened the night before – the biting, the kissing, how the grass felt under our bodies – but the body on the beach kept forcing itself to the front of my brain, obliterating everything else until I gave up pretending, told Mum I was going to the motel, pedalled like my backside was on fire and barged in on the vampires, dishevelled and ranting.

"Slow down and breathe," the Reverend repeated.

I opened my mouth to shout again.

"Hello, Gorgeous." Severn's soft voice stopped me before I spoke. "What's all the ruckus?"

At the sound of his voice, all the anger and fear in my head unravelled and I fell into his arms in a flood of tears. Severn hugged me tight, rocking me slightly until the tears subsided to breathy gasps. Looking up at his face I saw his confusion mixed with his love and concern. With a muttered apology I pulled away and ran to the bathroom where I blew my snuffling nose and splashed water on my reddened eyes. By the time I felt composed enough to return, Severn had made me coffee in one of the generic white motel cups. With a weak smile that barely lifted the corners of his mouth, he held it out to me then pulled me gently onto the couch beside him, wrapping his arm around my shoulders.

"Now, start from the beginning," he said. "What's got you so upset?"

"That," I said, pointing to the newspaper that lay on the floor where I had dropped it. "The body on the beach – we know her. She's crew! On the last show, she was ASM on OP side."

"Judith? Joanie?" The Reverend tried to remember.

"Julia," I said. "But you're missing the point. She was one of the crew the last time you guys were here. When Tasha was killed. The last time the police were looking for Severn." I swivelled my body so I was facing him. "If they realise there is a connection to us, they are going to come looking for you again. And the first place they will look is my place. It won't take them long to figure out we are all working another show and they will turn up at Mona Vale with a warrant and take you away. This is serious."

Severn released my shoulder so he could lean forwards to pick up the paper, read the article then sprang to his feet to thrust the paper at the Reverend. He paced back and forth across the floor twice then stopped in front of the Reverend, rocking the top half of his body, his arms folded so tightly to his chest it looked like he was wearing a straitjacket.

"Shit. Shit, shit, shit. Riley's right. Shit."

"Calm down, everybody," the Rev said, standing up to place his arm on Severn's back. "Severn, you're doing that stress thing that you do. Stop rocking. Sit down, we'll work this out. I agree it's not good, but it's not a problem yet. If the worst happens and we've got to get out fast, we've always got our alternative Vatican passports, with diplomatic immunity, and the Lear jet is still parked up in a comfy hangar at the airport. We can be out of here in the time it takes to get to the airport and get it on a runway. But just to be on the safe side, Aiden, why don't you nip out there today and make sure it's fuelled up."

"Sure," Aiden agreed. "But we are getting so far ahead of ourselves. That show was months ago. It's not like she's working this one. The police aren't going to look for people she barely knew months ago. They're going to be looking at who she knows now and what she's been doing recently. They are going to be focussed on her family, her partner, if she has one, her workmates. It will take them months before they widen their search to anywhere near us and by then, Robin Hood will be finished and we will have flown away. You're both panicking for nothing. Hell, at least this proves I was right – it wasn't Mad Sally. I told you nobody'll ever find her."

Severn sat down beside me again but continued to rock, his

arms still clenched around his chest.

"So what are you suggesting? That we just sit and wait it out?" he asked.

"For now." "Yes." The Rev and Aiden answered at the same time. "But let's keep our ears to the ground," the Reverend continued. "Severn, instead of sitting rocking, turn your brain on and use your computer skills. Get searching. Riley, if she's part of your company's usual crew, is there anyone you can talk to? Can you find out what she was doing last Friday night?"

Seven and I gave each other looks that questioned the point of the Rev's orders. I shrugged.

"Don't be so negative," the Rev said, picking up on our lack of enthusiasm. "If nothing else it will keep you two focussed. Look, for all we know the police have already figured it out and arrested someone."

"Or she had a heart attack," Aiden interjected, picking up the paper and waving it at me when I started to disagree. "It says it in here. The police are thinking it's natural causes." He waved the paper at Severn, "You dumb arse, they're not looking for anyone. They think she just dropped dead. Get a grip!"

"I'll talk to Mum," I said. I gulped down my coffee and reached forwards to put the empty cup on the floor at my feet. "She said Grant will want to go to the funeral, so I bet she's been phoning people madly this morning. If anyone can get the gossip, it'll be Mum. But I don't want to interrupt her yet. She'll need time to do the rounds of her urban spies." I turned to Severn, "You want to get out of here for a while?"

"Absolutely." He stopped rocking and unfolded his arms. "Give me a minute. There's no show tonight and you're dressed like a punter so I may as well play the same game. We can camouflage ourselves by not wearing black."

"A punter? What's wrong with my clothes?"

"Nothing. There's nothing with your clothes at all. You're clothes look wonderful. But they're blue. Blue jeans, white top. Not black. You look like an ordinary person, not crew. Just give me a minute to change and we can hide at the mall blending in with all the real ordinary people - the punters."

I sat and stared at the other two in stony silence while I waited for Severn to return. I had nothing left to say to them although I wondered if they had things they wanted to say to each other as the Rev's eyes flicked to me, to Aiden, back to me, to the door of

Sev's room and back to Aiden. Even I could read that code.

"We'll leave you to it," I said with a smile as Severn came back, looking very tasty in bum-caressing blue jeans and a long-sleeved but lightweight hoodie in a delicate dove grey that highlighted his blue eyes. Expensive grey high-top sneakers in a brand I can't afford finished off the outfit but as we closed the door behind us, he added one more item – a well-worn black, baker-boy cap.

"Protection against the sun," he explained as he pulled the brim down his forehead. "Now I know how hot it gets, I've learned my lesson. Where are we going?"

"I don't know," I laughed. "Just anywhere that isn't here. Let's walk."

Severn wrapped his arm around me, pulling me close, and we walked, my head resting sideways on his shoulder. Ahead of us three people waited at a bus stop, giving me an idea.

"Hey, I know where we can go." I pulled my metro card out of my pocket and held it up. "Let's go to a mall – just not the local one." I grabbed Severn's hand and pulled him towards the bus stop. While we waited, I sent a text message to Anita.

Wanna meet 7? We bussing to Northlands

Nobody looked at us as we boarded the bus, not even the driver who barely glanced as I swiped my metro card for both of us. We found seats half way back, surrounded by old ladies with shopping trolleys and young ones with folding prams and fractious babies.

"That'll be Anita soon," I said to Severn, as the woman in front of us juggled a squirming baby and a large bag.

"Rather her than me," Severn replied.

"Does it bother you? That you'll never..."

"Father a baby? Honestly? No. But that's just me. I've never clicked with children. But I know it bothers some of the others. Meredith, for one. She gets really weird around babies. I think she misses not being able to have one of her own."

"She's got Aiden as a twin brother – isn't that enough?"

"More than! What about you? I mean, would it be a problem that I can't ... that we couldn't? Well, at least not together. I mean, you could always ... um..."

"Oh shut up! No, okay, no, it's not a problem. It might even be a blessing. I'm not a baby person either. I know at some stage I have to go and meet my new half-sister in Australia but I'm trying to put it off until she can walk and talk. Secretly, and don't you ever tell her I said this, but between you and me, I hope I am always too busy to have to babysit for Anita." I clapped my hand to my mouth. "Oh, that sounds so mean."

I stared out the bus window while a question stirred inside my brain until I had to ask it.

"Hey, what happens if someone is pregnant when they get turned … into, you know…," I made small flappy wing motions with my hands.

Severn sat back in his seat and moved his left hand across his chest and his right to his chin in a classic thinking pose. I watched with amusement as he tried to process an answer. His mouth opened and closed, his eyebrows raised, one at a time, then furrowed down, then rose again together. Finally he spluttered out an answer.

"I have no idea. Good question though."

"I wonder if it would depend on how far along the mother was," I pondered. "I mean, if a baby's born early, there's a cut-off point before which it can't survive. I wonder if there's something similar?"

"I guess there are only three possibilities," Severn said. "Either it's like a cancer or other growth that is 'cured' at the change," he made inverted commas with his fingers as he said the word cured, "and she would lose the baby and not be pregnant any more, or she would have a normal baby or," he made flappy wing motions like I had, "she would have a … special baby. But I don't know what the answer is because I don't know of it ever happening. Although, if there are more of us out there somewhere, then it could have."

"Here's a scary thought." My brain was racing. "If you stay the same age when you change, would a changed baby ever grow? Wouldn't it be a newborn for ever?"

"Now that would suck!"

CHAPTER SEVEN

Anita met us by the computer store. Or rather she met me outside but Severn was inside, shopping like my mother.

"Where is he?" she asked as she ran towards me. "Come on! You can't call me to meet him then hide him away. I want to see this guy."

"He's in there shopping," I pointed to the computer store. "I couldn't stand it any more. If I hear one more question about migs, gigs and killer bites I'll scream. Yes, before you ask, he's a geek. I've told you that. Probably more of a geek than Caleb."

"But a cute one, I presume? If you're not into him for his computer skills, he must have some other attractions."

"Oh hell yes." I pointed to two men standing by a shelf of cables. "That's Severn over there. The one in the grey hoodie."

"Oookaaay," Anita said, twisting her head to look him up and down from a variety of angles. "Yes, I can see why he appeals. He's not Tasha's type though, so she must have been just stirring you up."

"That failed."

Anita gave me the same sweeping inspection she had just given Severn.

"You look different. Yesterday you weren't too happy but now ....oh slap me! You left my place to meet him in some dark, secluded place. Did you two ...? You did, didn't you?"

"You just shut up. All I will say is that the Edmonds Gardens are nicer than the school garden. Now shut up! This is not a matter for discussion."

"It'll keep. Now introduce me to your man before he buys the entire shop."

I knew Severn had heard every word of our conversation as he looked up as she spoke and walked towards us, smiling and holding up a small bag.

"See, just two cables and a couple of connectors. No laptops, no monitors, no new computers at all, even though Grant really needs to upgrade his. Okay, I might have been tempted but not at those prices. I can get everything way cheaper in France. Hi, you must be Anita. I'm Severn." Severn held out his free hand which Anita grabbed with both of hers.

"Wow!" She looked him up and down unashamedly, turned to me and nodded. "Yeah. I'd buy that."

Severn gave us both one of his patented looks where he lowers his head then looks over the top of his glasses. That expression usually means he is about to say something sarcastic, so I leapt in before he could, grabbing their still connected hands and making a show of pulling them apart and returning Anita's hands to beside her body.

"Sorry, girl, but you can't buy him, he's not for sale. How about I buy us an ice cream instead?"

I was relieved to see Severn's next reaction was to laugh. Still sniggering, he put his arm around me and kissed me on the top of my head as I steered us in the direction of the specialty ice cream shop. Funny how it was the only shop in the place I could find blindfolded. Anita went for a double chocolate, I couldn't make up my mind so had two scoops of different flavours, and Severn settled for a single scoop of vanilla.

"Where are you from?" Anita asked as we ambled around the mall, licking our ice creams as we walked. "I mean, I know you've been in France 'cos Riley told me but you're not French to start with, are you? You've got some sort of accent but it's hardly there and I can't figure out what it is."

"I was born in Scotland," Severn answered. "But if I ever had a Scottish accent, I lost it years ago. I've been away from there for a long time."

"You must have left when you were a baby," Anita said. "Mum has a friend who's from Glasgow and, even though she's lived here for most of her life, her accent's still so thick you could cut it with a knife."

I could tell Severn was thinking hard about his answer. He could hardly say he was 19 when he left after he had just said he'd been away for years, and he definitely couldn't say those years added up to a hundred and ten.

"Yeah, left young, moved around a lot. My accent, if I've got one now, is probably a lot of different ones. I don't know, I can't hear myself. What about you? I'm guessing your accent's genuine Kiwi - your vowels are flatter than Riley's Australian ones."

"Yeah, born and bred local, me," Anita replied. "The furthest we've moved is from one side of Christchurch to another, and that was only a year and a half ago. Ask Riley where she's from."

"I know where she's from. We've had that conversation. She's from Brisbane."

"Yeah but make her say it. Go on."

"Why?"

"Oh, just because. Okay, it cracks me up the way she says it. We say Bris-bin. She says Breeze-bane. Cracks me up every time."

"Bitch!" I cursed her but with a smile to show I didn't mean it.

"See – beech, like the tree. Or the seaside. Love it."

Great. Gee thanks, Anita, remind me about the beach.

"Speaking of Australia," I said, "I've decided what I'm doing this year."

"You're going to go and live with your dad?" The way she screwed her nose up as she spoke showed what Anita thought of that idea.

"No, exactly the opposite. I have decided definitely not to go to Oz. I'm going to go to MAINZ for the year."

"Maine? You're going to America?" Severn sounded horrified.

"No, silly, not Maine, MAINZ – the place that teaches sound engineering. If I'm going to end up behind a sound desk, I need to know what I'm doing and why I'm doing it. I'll come off it with a certificate and, with the practical experience I've been getting, I should be able to get theatre work anywhere."

"And come touring with us," Severn said, his smile widening. "Is that in the plans?"

"I'm hoping that's in the plan," I said, looking up at Severn so my face was masked from Anita. "I can see myself touring." I added a whispered "forever" and caught Severn's quick intake of breath as he heard it. For a brief second his eyes brightened, flickered, and I saw his muscles tense, vampire senses triggering, but he was quick to recover, scratching his head and resetting his baker-boy cap to pull himself back. In control again, he winked at me then made a show of looking at his watch. Anita thought she was being given a hint.

"Do you guys have to be somewhere?"

"No, sorry, force of habit."

"Hey, I've got an idea," Anita said, oblivious to Severn's fight for self-control. "If you guys don't have a show tonight, why don't we all go to the movies? Caleb and I were going anyway – why don't you two come with us?"

I looked at Severn who shrugged his shoulders and looked

sweetly geeky, his eyes back to their normal shade of blue.

"Yeah, okay," I said. "What are we going to see?"

"You guys get to vote. We haven't decided. I want to see the sad one set in World War Two but Caleb wants to see the horror movie with vampires and werewolves. He's got a thing about werewolves. They're his pet research subject."

"I vote for werewolves," Severn said with an evil grin. "Not into them myself but vampires make good theatre." He gave me that over-the-glasses look again.

"I vote for werewolves too," I said. "I'm into vampires although a werewolf could be more use, especially if I could teach it to retrieve."

Anita sighed in resignation. "Okay, werewolves it is. I'm going to meet Caleb now, so we'll meet you guys upstairs at the cinema. Movie starts at 8.30."

She was already texting madly on her phone as she walked away so I wasn't surprised to hear my phone ping in my pocket. The message made me laugh. I held up my phone to show Severn the string of smiley faces, some with hearts in their eyes, one wearing glasses like Severn's, lots of hearts, thumbs-up and even a unicorn.

"I think she likes you," I said.

"I like her too. She's slightly nuts. Anyway, we've got a few hours to kill – what can I tempt you into doing?"

"Your place or mine?"

"Both. Your place, junk food, movie, my place."

"Let's go."

CHAPTER EIGHT

Mum wasn't home. She had left me a note saying she was meeting Grant when he finished work and they were going to a restaurant for dinner, and she left me a twenty-dollar note to buy myself a take-away. Perfect. I drew my bedroom curtains and for the next hour, Severn and I discovered each other's bodies, stroking, caressing, kissing, loving. I asked him to bite me but he refused, teasing me instead with licks and nibbles.

We showered together, Severn's extended fangs driving me crazy as he ran them over my wet shoulders. I wanted to stroke his wings, to feel the soft leather, but he moved my hands away, keeping his wings tightly furled and only unfurling them slightly afterwards so he could carefully pat them dry. His wings were still a no-touch area.

I scribbled "Thanks, gone to the movies" over Mum's note as we left, the money tucked in my jacket pocket and Severn's cap now on my head, keeping my loose, flowing hair in place against the developing nor'west wind. We walked, arms entwined around each other, to the bus stop but as we passed the neighbour's house, Severn stopped. His head swivelled as if he was listening for something, then he shook his head and started walking again.

"What was that?" I asked.

"I don't know. I thought I saw someone, behind that house, and I was sure I heard footsteps, but they disappeared and it was so fast I must have been mistaken. Might have been a cat."

"Oh okay," Why didn't I tell him about the figure I had seen flashes of? That I thought was Aiden? Maybe it still was. Maybe he was watching us again. Then we saw the bus coming so we had to run and I forgot all about it.

Once we reached the mall, my first stop was the food court – I was ravenous. Anita and Caleb found us there, tucking into burgers and chips, upsized to large, an ice cream sundae (okay, that was just for me) and black coffee to wash it all down. Severn showed his age (his real age) by leaping up as they approached and pulling out a chair for Anita, then offering his hand to Caleb.

"Hi, you must be Caleb. It's a pleasure to meet you. I'm

Severn, spelt with an R, like the river."

Caleb shook hands then sat while Anita have me a wide-mouthed, silent "oh" behind her hand. Guys our age don't normally have manners like that, and if they did, they wouldn't use them with us in a mall food court.

"Can I get you anything?" Severn asked them.

"No, no thanks," Caleb stuttered. "We've eaten. Healthy salads at my place, although burgers and chips seems more appropriate for vampires."

Severn's head jolted up. "What?"

"We're not vampires," I said quickly.

"Speak for yourself," Severn replied, "I might be."

"Bite me."

"I meant," Caleb regained control of the conversation, "burgers, red meat, seem more appropriate than lettuce before we watch a movie about vampires and werewolves."

"Or pizza." Severn was grinning. "As a vampire, I have to say I prefer pizza. Or chocolate."

"Vampires don't eat pizza," Anita argued. "They don't eat anything, except blood."

"Says who?" Severn was enjoying this too much. "Blood through chocolate. Yum."

Anita turned to me. "No wonder you two got together. You're as weird as each other."

The movie was dark, gritty and violent. The one thing it wasn't was scary. At least, not to me. Beside me Anita jumped, squealed and hid her face in Caleb's chest at all the right times, but I struggled not to laugh. Severn was having a harder job and had to resort to faking a coughing fit as a cover when the vampire revealed himself to the heroine, flashing his CGI'd canine teeth to protect her from the approaching pack of werewolves.

Severn's mood changed as the movie reached the dramatic 'bite' scene. As the on-screen vampire stroked the heroine's hair back from her lily-white neck, Severn matched him, gently sweeping my hair to the side. Both vampires lowered their heads at the same time. The movie vampire bit, the heroine screamed, Anita squealed and I felt the point of a tooth on my skin. I wriggled away.

"Stop it! Later," I whispered.

There was no answer except a ragged breath. A quick glance sideways told me Severn was, for the second time today, fighting to restrain his natural urges. If we hadn't been sitting beside my friends, in a crowded movie theatre, I might have offered him my neck and said "go for it" – it's not like I didn't want him to bite me – but I had no idea what my reaction might be, what the bite might lead to. I needed to be somewhere private before I found out.

By the end of the movie, Severn was back in innocent teenager mode but I could tell that wasn't going to last long. On the bus journey home he kept touching my hair and running his finger along my neck. I assumed, I hoped, we would go to his motel but, as we neared my stop, he pushed the button to halt the bus. We walked silently down the dark street and as we rounded the corner into our side street, he stopped and pulled me close, his breath warm on my neck. I flicked my hair sideways to offer my neck but he drew back.

"Bite me."

"No, I can't."

"Why? I want you to. In the movies, I wasn't saying don't bite me, I was saying not there, not in the movie theatre. Not in public. But I wanted you to. So do it now, bite me."

Severn held me at arm's length, his eyes sparkling hunter bright, his extended fangs white against the darkness. "I can't."

"Why not? What have I done?"

"I can't because I need to feed. Badly. And I'm scared that if I bite you, I won't stop. I'll drink too much."

"Oh." Who would have thought that having a vampire refuse to bite you would be so crushingly disappointing. Rejection plus. I understood. I was even grateful that he cared enough not to want to risk it, but damn it, I wanted him to bite me. It felt so damned good. Severn seemed to understand.

"I'm going to get you home, then I'm going to go, hunt, feed. Leave your window open. I'll be back when I'm not dangerous."

Deflated and getting cold, I let him walk me to my door. I could feel the change in his energy as he moved – he was in full hunting mode, twitching at every sound – which is why he saw the shadow before I did. I spotted it as we turned into our driveway. I looked sideways at Severn to catch his attention but he was already watching, listening, tracking whatever it was. I tried to talk, to tell him I had seen it before, but he raised a finger to his lips, motioning me to be quiet. We stood, silently searching the darkness, for what seemed like an eternity but eventually Severn relaxed, kissed me on my forehead and pushed me towards the door.

"Later," he promised. I caught a flash of white fang in his smile as he spun on his heel and sprinted away, leaving me no option except to go inside where I knew Mum and Grant would be waiting.

They were, but the conversation was brief. I merely waved, smiled and called a cheery "good night," as I kept walking towards my room.

Severn licking my neck woke me up. I began to roll from my side, where I had been curled up, onto my back to take him into my arms, but he placed his hand on my shoulder to stop me, holding me on my side so my neck was exposed. Severn's tongue searched across my skin, finding the right spot, then he bit, hard, sharp, without warning. I yelped, then made myself relax and accept the pulsing sting. I wanted to reach the ecstasy of my first bite but this was different. It felt warm, comfortable, addictive. The gentle rhythm of Severn drinking wove a spell I didn't want to break. Again, it seemed to end too quickly. It felt so good – it would be so easy to let him bleed me to death. Then he was tucking my blanket around my chin and kissing me goodbye, leaving me with more questions than answers.

CHAPTER NINE

In the morning I was too tired to move. All I wanted to do was lie in bed. When I finally tried to get up, a dizzy spell hit me and I had to lie down again before I was sick. I tried again and made it to the bathroom where I had to sit on the edge of the bath to stop myself fainting. I sat for a minute, willing myself not to vomit. When I had regained control, I pulled myself to my feet and staggered to the mirror. I looked like death.

"Bloody hell, Severn, what have you done to me?"

I glared at the white, colourless face staring back at me from the mirror. Even my normally red lips were pale. I lifted my hair to check my neck. The tiny spots from the first bite had almost disappeared but on the other side of my neck the bite from last night had bruised. I was sure Mum would see it and I didn't know how I was going to explain it.

I crept back to my bed and pulled the covers over my head. Maybe if I had another hour's sleep I would jump out of bed full of enthusiasm and raring to go. Who was I kidding? I wondered if Mum would let me stay in bed all day.

I was asleep when Mum knocked on my door an hour later. I must have still looked pale as she took one look at me and ordered me to stay in bed for the day. That was fine by me – it wasn't like I had any plans. The boys had been out hunting so there was no point going to the motel as they would be sleeping and, although I loved spending time with Anita, there were questions I didn't want to get into with her – well, not until I figured out what answers I could safely give her.

I wasted most of the day alternately dozing and eating food that Mum brought me at regular intervals but by mid afternoon I was bored. An attempt at sitting up showed my blood levels must have improved as I managed to remain upright without wanting to faint or vomit, so I decided to try walking to the kitchen for coffee. Mum looked up from the dress she was ironing.

"Feeling better, dear?" she asked.

"Yeah, a bit, thanks."

"What brought that on? You were fine yesterday."

"I don't know," I lied. "I think the stress of sorting out the sound in the show, and then Tommy's kidnapping, finally got to me. As soon as we got time off, I think my body just turned itself off. But I'm feeling better now."

"Well, take it easy for the rest of the day. Don't overdo it. Oh, by the way, Julia's funeral is tomorrow morning. Are you coming?"

"Definitely." I wasn't going to miss any chance to find out what really happened to her on the beach.

Thoughts of the beach gave me a purpose for the rest of the afternoon – I needed to find out more about the other Brighton bodies that the Reverend had referred to and tried to pass off as nothing. Time to search the internet.

For the next hour I searched for everything I could find on bodies on beaches with Brighton in their name and I was horrified at the number, of Brightons as well as bodies. I found forty three Brightons around the world and a deeper search found bodies on beaches in Brightons in England, Australia and South Africa as well as the ones here. Three men and five women. The body count was growing.

If I hoped the Reverend would give me some more details, I was wrong. Instead, when I let myself into the motel that evening, all I received was an angry tirade.

"Why did you let him bite you?" the Reverend greeted me. "Let me see." He grabbed my hair and pulled it away from my neck, revealing the spots on one side and the fresh bruises on the other. "Damn it. Riley, you can't let him do this."

"Why not? If I don't mind, what's the problem?"

"Severn!" The Reverend yelled towards Sev's door. "Get out here!"

"What's the matter?" Severn muttered as he came out of his room, rubbing his eyes and yawning. "Oh, hi Riley, sorry, I was asleep."

I was stopped from crossing the room to give him a hug by the Reverend who stepped between us. "Sit, you two, and listen up. This is important." We sat. "Severn, you cannot, cannot, feed off Riley, and Riley, you cannot let him bite you."

"Why?" I asked. I was confused but Severn just looked angry at the Rev who stood in front of us, hands on his hips, prepared to lecture.

"Let me ask you how you feel, Riley? No, let me tell you, because I bet I know. By those marks, you've been bitten twice so, let's see, the first felt euphoric, you wanted more, but I am betting that last night it made you feel sleepy, calm, and today you felt like crap. Am I close?"

"Yes," I was forced to agree. "Actually you're spot on, That's exactly how I felt. But so what? If I know what to expect, why are you saying Sev can't bite me?"

"Yeah," Severn sulked. "You can't tell us what to do."

"No, I can't," the Reverend continued, "but I can tell you what's happening, what's going to happen if you continue. Then, when you have heard me out, you can do whatever you want, but at least I will have done my best. Riley, as you know we have to hunt to feed, so we have a few tricks up our sleeve to make that easier. We need our meals to let us feed, not to fight back, and to do that our fangs contain drugs."

"What? Venom? Like snakes?" I glared at Severn. "Have you poisoned me? Am I going to die?"

"No," the Reverend was quick to assure me. "You won't die, if you stop now. But here's the problem, like any drugs, ours are addictive."

"Hang on a minute," Severn interrupted. "Go back to the one day euphoric, next day sleepy bit. Riley, you said that's what happened to you, so how did you know, David?"

"Because of how you were, Severn, and because of how it works. Riley, I'm not belittling your relationship with Severn, I know you two really do care for each other, but what happened to you happens to everyone we bite. We want them to be compliant, and the blood to flow, so with the first bite we inject a small amount of a drug that enhances the experience. That's why I am betting you felt wonderful."

"Yes, I did."

"But last night Severn, you were hungry, right? After you two had been to the movies, Severn, you came back here and you were in hunting mode. I could tell as soon as you walked in. So I knew you hadn't fed off Riley again and I applaud you for that. You came out with us and, without inflicting Riley with the details, we hunted and we fed well. Then you went back to Riley, Severn. Am I right?"

"Yes," Severn agreed reluctantly. "So what?"

"That's the other side of the drug, and it's affected by how we feel, not how the person we bite feels. Severn, you were well fed, so you would have been starting to feel tired and when we are in that mood, the drug in our fangs changes. When we need sleep, our guard drops and we risk being overpowered. To avoid that, to avoid being the victim of our victim, the drug we inject changes to a sedative which is why I was betting Riley felt lethargic afterwards. And finally, Riley, you look pale, so I am guessing that being bitten twice in two days has taken its toll. You've lost too much blood. You are going to need a few days to recover fully."

"Okay, I get that," I said, "but what did you mean about the drugs being addictive?"

"They're drugs," the Rev explained, "and like any drugs, if you keep taking them, you will become an addict, you won't be able to function without your fix. A few hundred years ago, that worked well for us. Villages full of keen, faithful peasants, getting their religious highs by letting winged angels drink their life force. But it doesn't work as well now. Riley, if you keep getting bitten, even if you enjoy it, you will constantly be taking in drugs that make you euphoric one day then drugs that make you tired the next. Uppers and downers. And like anyone who takes drugs, you will very quickly become an addict, with all the usual problems a drug addict has. I'm sure you have better plans for your life than ending up in a gutter."

"I wouldn't let it get that far," Severn argued.

"How would you stop it? The same way Seth did with Meredith and Olivia? Turn her?"

"What if I want him to turn me?" I asked, my belligerent tone getting a sneer from the Rev as a response.

"No, you don't," he growled. "Not under these circumstances anyway. Look, Riley, we know you've spent the last few months wondering if you were turning, and I can see why you might still be considering it, but if you do, it has to be a sensible, well-thought-out decision. It can't be because you have become an incurable addict and it's change or die. That's not happening on my watch."

"Yeah, you're right," Severn agreed. "That's not happening on my watch either. Sorry, David, and sorry, Riley, I wasn't thinking."

CHAPTER TEN

"That's blown away what I came here to talk about," I said. "Okay, Rev, I hear you. I am picking up what you're putting down. I will be more careful. We," I put my hand on Severn's knee to include him, "will be more careful. I felt ghastly this morning and I couldn't figure out why. Well, I knew it was because of the bites but it didn't make sense that I felt so good one day and so awful the next, so thanks for the heads-up. Sev, I love you a lot but I'm not stupid enough to become a vampire junkie."

"Sorry," Severn said, a small smile and one half-raised eyebrow begging my forgiveness. "But I genuinely didn't know this stuff either." With a sudden angry shove, he propelled himself off the couch to tower over the shorter Reverend, matching the Rev's hands on hips stance and dropping his voice to a menacing growl. "It's your fault. I am actually really, really sick of your education policy for new vampire converts. It sucks big time!"

The Reverend opened and closed his mouth a couple of times to form a reply but Severn continued, his voice getting louder with every word.

"When I was turned, and for the next one hundred plus years, I had a problem with Seth and those nasty, bitchy girls. You were there and you did nothing. For one hundred and ten years you watched them bully me every way they could. And you did nothing. Nothing! Back then I thought that was because Seth was the boss and you were just as low on the totem pole as me. Then, just a few months ago, I find out that you are actually the boss. Not just of this team but the boss of the whole guild, the Grand Master. You could have stopped Seth decades ago but you didn't. Just like you didn't bother to explain to me about the drugs in our fangs – information I should have had, especially as Seth made me the hunter for the team. David, would you care to explain why, with seven hundred years' experience at being a Grand Master, you suck so badly at teaching us what we need to know."

Severn remained glaring down at the Reverend until the Rev hung his head and moved away, walking to the small kitchen before returning to face Severn. He opened his mouth to speak, closed it again and retraced his steps through the kitchen and back to us.

"You're right. You're absolutely right. Unlike Seth, I never had any ambition to be Grand Master. The only reason the Council voted me into the role when Father Albrecht decided to step down was because I own the monastery and the land it's on – not because I have the qualifications to be a good Grand Master. To be honest, one of the reasons I agreed to keep an eye on Seth and not stay back at Montagne des Anges, being Grand Master, was because I know Albrecht, Arnaud and Maurice can all do a much better job of running the place, and teaching new recruits, than I can. That's where I failed with you, Severn. When Seth first turned you, I should have intervened. I should have taken you aside, explained what was going on and sent you back to the monastery to learn this stuff. I failed completely and for that, I sincerely apologise. Yes, you need proper training, and so do I – in how to be a Grand Master worthy of the title."

He held out his hand and, after a thoughtful hesitation, Severn accepted and shook it.

"Okay," I interjected, "Let's all agree that we've all made mistakes but I didn't come here for an intervention. If you think we're not being careful, I think someone else has a similar but bigger problem. Where's Aiden?"

"Out, why?"

"Brighton beaches, and things left on them. What has Aiden been up to and why are you covering up for him?"

"Covering up? For Aiden?" The Reverend sounded genuinely surprised.

"Yeah," I replied, "I reckon you are. I've been on the computer searching Brighton beach and bodies – there are a few more than you've been admitting to. Have you guys been to South Africa?"

"Yes, four times," the Rev admitted. "What are you getting at?"

"Bodies on beaches named Brighton – I found eight of them – in England, Australia, here and in South Africa – all places you guys have been. Coincidence? Convince me!"

"Show me," Severn interjected. "I need to see this."

"Sure," I said. "But make it tomorrow. Right now I'm chock full of information that I need time to process. In the meantime, maybe you can convince the great Grand Master to let you in on what he and Aiden have been up to behind your back."

Not waiting for an answer, I walked out, slammed the door

behind me, rescued my bike that was still locked to the fence from yesterday, and pedalled home, thankful that the wind in my face was keeping me alert as Severn's drugs in my system were still making me dizzy if I moved my head too quickly.

At home Mum and Grant were discussing their plans for tomorrow which gave me a good excuse to join in and ask if they had heard anything about what happened to Julia.

"Apparently she drowned," Mum said. "It was on the news. What they can't figure out is how she got to the beach where she was found. The police are asking for information from anyone who might have seen her travelling to the beach or walking along it."

"They found her car," Grant added. "It was still at her house, so she didn't drive to the beach."

"She might have driven with someone else," Mum suggested.

"Or taken a bus," I said.

"That's why the police are calling for witnesses," Grant said.

"So there were no marks on her?" I asked.

"I suppose not, if she drowned," Grant said.

"I doubt they would put that sort of detail in the paper," Mum pointed out.

"What sort of marks were you thinking of?" Grant asked. "Have you heard something we haven't?"

"No, no. I ... um ... it's all just so strange, isn't it? I mean, it's a wide, flat beach. And it was Julia. She's the last person I would have expected to even go to the beach, let alone drown there. She hated swimming."

"How did you know that?" Mum asked.

"We talked about it one night at the show. One of the dancers was saying how he had bought a new surfboard and I remember Julia saying she couldn't swim and there was no way she would ever go in the sea. Apparently she had nearly drowned when she was a kid and was still scared of the water. So it's a bit weird that they found her at the beach."

"But it explains why she drowned," Grant said. "If she couldn't swim."

"But why was she there at all? And at night?"

"Romance," Mum declared. "Why else would a young woman be walking along the beach in the moonlight?"

"If there was somebody with her, how come she drowned? Wouldn't they have saved her? Or at least called for help? And why were there no footprints on the sand?" I asked.

"Those are probably all questions the police are asking," Grant said. "Maybe we'll hear some answers tomorrow at the funeral."

As I wasn't going to give them my opinion as to why there were no footprints near her body, I said goodnight and left them pondering the questions I had asked. I was genuinely tired and was nearly asleep when I heard the determined tap on my window. What did Severn want that couldn't wait? Shelving a few ungracious and unloving thoughts, I rolled out of bed and opened the window without really looking at who was on the other side so I was shocked when it was Aiden who climbed in.

"What do you want?" I demanded.

"I want to talk to you. I want to know what your problem is with me? For the last few days, since I sorted out the Mad Sally issue, you seem to have decided I am some kind of crazed killer. Why? What have I done to you?"

"To me, nothing I can prove but you're not denying killing Sally, are you?"

"That was business. The Reverend told me to clean up, so I did."

"Exactly! Couldn't you just have paid her off, like the Rev said you were going to do?"

"Oh, don't be so naive. If we had paid her money she would have taken it, waited a while then kidnapped the kid again, or kept asking for more money. The way I cleaned up, your friends the McCormacks can get back to their lives with no possibility of her ruining it. Clean. Tidy. But that doesn't make me dangerous, just sensible, and it doesn't make me responsible for every person in the city who dies while we are here helping you out of your amateur theatre mess."

"Wow! Tell me how you really feel. If you didn't want to help me, why did you come."

"Oh get a grip, I didn't say I didn't want to come, I'm just pointing out that I am not to blame for everything bad that happens while we are here. So can you lay off badmouthing me to the Rev?"

"Only if you stop following me around. It's creepy."

"Following you? When? I haven't followed you. Why would I waste good hunting time doing that?"

"Then who has? The Rev?"

Aiden's sat on the end of my bed. He was still tense but his anger had diffused into concern.

"What do you mean someone has been following you? When and where?"

"All sorts of places." I described the times I had thought I had seen a figure and why I assumed it had been Aiden because of its speed. When I added that Severn had seen it too, Aiden reacted, moving from the bed to the window in one fluid stride. Without an explanation he climbed through the window and ran off into the darkness. I watched him disappear, closed the window and returned to bed but, although I was desperate for it, sleep was a long time coming.

CHAPTER ELEVEN

Julia's funeral was beautiful but sad. Our stage manager spoke about Julia's work backstage and one of the younger chorus members sang her favourite song. Grant made a short speech as president of the company, even though he didn't know her very well. I looked for Beth, who had been the other ASM on our last show, and we hugged as if Julia had been our best friend.

Afterwards, we joined the crowd in a nearby hall, nibbling savouries and sharing memories. I wandered around, listening to conversations, hoping to hear something more about how she died, but either nobody knew anything or they weren't saying. The only information I gleaned was that everybody was surprised she had been at the beach as her fear of water was well known. It wasn't until I had given up on hearing anything useful that I hit the jackpot. I was reaching for another sausage roll when I heard the stage manager's voice.

"I don't think she had a current boyfriend," I heard her say in reply to a question from the woman next to her who I recognised from our wardrobe department. "Not since the show. She was pretty cut up about that and it was pretty unfair what he did to her."

"What happened?" the wardrobe lady asked. "Did someone let her down?"

"In a big way. That gorgeous hunk of flyman who came in with the travelling crew, Seth Borman. He flirted with her backstage every night and in the second week she was all excited because he had taken her out after the show. According to her it was all on, then he packed up and left with the rest of the crew and she never heard from him again. Not a word. As far as I know she hadn't dated anybody since then."

Seth! She was one of Seth's conquests. Did the Reverend know that?

"Didn't he even say goodbye?" the wardrobe lady asked. "The rotten ... oh I shouldn't swear at a funeral ... but what a mean thing to do."

At least none of the stage crew, except the vampires and me, knew what had really happened to Seth. The stage manager obviously thought he had just been sleazy and done a bunk, which meant the vampires must have done a good job of cleaning the stage after I left.

Seth and Julia. I hadn't picked that but I wasn't on Julia's side of the stage during the show and Seth was mostly up in the fly tower, so he must have made his move when he passed her to go up and down the tower's ladder. I wouldn't have thought Julia was Seth's type, but I guess she was – I mean she walked, breathed and had a body full of blood, so that probably covered all the essentials. Every time I had seen him, he was surrounded by his acolytes, Meredith and Olivia. I wondered if they knew about Julia and what they had thought about her.

"It looks as if they have written it off as suicide," Grant said on the drive home.

"Suicide?" Mum gasped in horror. "I thought they had decided she drowned. Some kind of accident."

"She drowned all right, there's no doubt about that, but I was talking to her father and he said Julia had been depressed lately over some guy who loved her and left her. They haven't figured out how she got to the beach but from what her father said, the parents just want to be left to grieve. They want the police to let it go."

"That's sad," Mum said. I stayed quiet, thinking of Seth. I hoped it wasn't suicide – I didn't want to think our actions to save ourselves had caused her death.

Mum broke the silence by declaring that funerals were too sad and she needed cheering up. Grant knew the solution without asking and changed the car's direction to drop us off at the nearest mall. With a rueful smile, he handed Mum his credit card and told her to call when we needed a ride home. Mum had Grant well trained.

Clothes shops – the mall had lots of clothes shops and Mum worked her way through all of them, swiping the strip off Grant's credit card and loading me up with an assortment of labelled bags. We shopped our way along the ground floor and when we reached our favourite coffee shop in this particular mall, I begged Mum to take a break. I fell into a chair, dumped the pile of parcels on the floor around me and let Mum fetch a large, soy cappuccino with cinnamon for herself and a mochaccino with whipped cream for me.

"I had another letter from your father today," Mum said between delicate sips of her coffee. "He has calmed down a bit since you promised to go over there as soon as you could, but he is still blaming me and claiming I have brainwashed you."

"Oh, really? He needs to get over himself. Tell you what, I will email him and say I will definitely come over at Easter if he pays for the tickets. I will tell him I am enrolling at MAINZ and send him the Easter holiday dates so he understands I will only be there for a few days. Hopefully that will be enough and he will stop hassling us."

"You're really not interested in meeting the baby, are you?"

"Nope, not at all, until it's old enough to walk and talk. Horrid big sister, aren't I?"

"Well, as I keep telling him, you're not a kid anymore and you are more than capable of making your own decisions. I'm sure in his head you are still at primary school." She paused and we sipped our coffees in perfect unison like synchronised swimmers. "Tomorrow, if you like, we could find out what you need to do to enrol in your course. The show isn't until the evening so we have all day to organise the paperwork. How does that sound?"

"That sounds perfect," I said, smiling over my cup.

"What does Severn think of your plan? Have you told him yet?"

"Yes, I told him and Anita at the same time. Sev's all for it. I think the Reverend knows the guys who run the course so I reckon he will give me a good reference if I need one."

"I'm sure he will," Mum agreed before she dropped into the sweet tone that instantly warns me to listen very carefully to all the hidden levels of what she will say next. "If you join their crew and tour with them after you finish your course, you are going to be away for a very long time, aren't you? It's going to be a major change to your lifestyle."

She was doing that I-know-they-are-vampires thing again. I needed to choose my words just as selectively.

"Wherever I go with them, I will still only be a plane-ride away. I'm not sure yet if I will travel with them for a while to gain more theatre experience or whether I will join them permanently. I realise that joining permanently will be a huge move, so I won't be making that decision lightly. It's not like there is any rush."

I thought I had worded that well and fended off Mum's usual snide retaliatory remark, as she finished her coffee and suggested we set off again on her shop-till-she-dropped mission, but as we passed a pharmacy she threw in the curve-ball I thought I had avoided.

"If you were turned into a vampire young enough, you'd never need plastic surgery to stay beautiful."

"Only if you were beautiful before you changed," I replied. "Ugly would stay ugly."

"You'll be fine."

Did I say my mother was some kind of a witch?

Mum ran out of steam half way around the mall's top floor, plonked herself down on a convenient bench seat and sent Grant a text to pick us up. We made our way to the pick-up point and perched on a planter box to wait, enjoying the warmth of the sun on our faces.

"You might miss this, though," she said without warning. "How is Severn? He didn't cope too well in the sun at the matinee. Still, he did better than I would have expected. Would a high factor sunscreen help? Or one of those Australian bush hats with the wide brim?"

I was saved from having to answer by the toot of a car horn - Grant, in the role of knight on a white horse, riding to my rescue. I hustled Mum and her parcels to the loading zone where we collapsed gratefully into the car to let Grant chauffeur us home. He had an old musical playing through the cd player which made Mum automatically burst into song. Grant picked up the men's lines and I even offered a few chorus notes – anything to avoid more of Mum's disturbing conversations.

CHAPTER TWELVE

"I don't know how to deal with her," I moaned to Severn later as we sat on the Edmonds Gardens grass, gazing up at the night sky.

"Maybe we should come clean and just tell her. Maybe I should take off my shirt and show her my wings."

"Maybe you should. I think she's testing me, testing us, to see how long we will keep up pretending you guys are human."

"What do you want to do?"

"Tomorrow. Mum suggested we do my MAINZ enrolment tomorrow. Why don't you come over. I'll bet you a pizza that she brings up the subject. I reckon we call her bluff and tell her the truth."

"I wish Aiden would tell me the truth. I know he's lying about something. Him and the Rev. They've gone out again tonight, together. They're not hunting, it's too early for that, but they were huddled up together before they left, writing notes to each other so I couldn't hear what they were talking about. When they left, they both looked really serious, so something is up, but they're not letting me in on whatever it is."

"Aiden came and saw me last night," I said. "He wasn't happy. He accused me of badmouthing him to the Rev, which I have to admit was true, but when I told him to stop following me, he denied it and, you know what, I believed him."

"You've had someone following you? When?"

"Several times. Like when I was going from my place to your motel, or home again. Like I told Aiden, I never saw who it was but they moved so fast, I assumed it was Aiden. You guys are the only ones I know who can be that stealthy."

Severn didn't answer. He sat straighter, pulled his knees up, wrapped his arms around them protectively and rocked his body backwards and forwards. Finally he looked at me over the rim of his glasses and spoke.

"Moving fast. You see a flash that's so quick you can't tell if it was coloured clothing or a black shadow, but you're sure it's too big to be a cat or a bird. Yeah, I've seen it too. But Aiden wasn't who I thought it was. For a brief second, yesterday, I thought I recognised the shape, but I can't be right. I can't be. Honestly, I wish it had been Aiden. Him, I could deal with."

"So who is it?" I asked.

"Someone it can't possibly be. Look, sorry, I know tonight was supposed to be about us, but I need to find the others. I need to find out if they are thinking the same thing I am, or if they already know and are covering it up, because, if that's the case, I am going to lose my rag and things could get violent. Come on, I'll walk you home."

"No you won't! Whoever, whatever, this is, it's been following me for days and it's been creeping me out. I want to know the answer, and there is no way I am going to sit quietly at home like a good little girl while you yomp off on a secret mission. Wherever you're going, I'm going too. Anyway, someone has to stop you and Aiden from killing each other because the Rev won't – he'll just wait until you've both gasped your last breath, then clean up the evidence. So where will they be? Where do we look first?"

Severn looked from me to himself, fingering the blue denim of his jeans.

"First we get out of these clothes."

"Um," I misinterpreted the intent of his words and he laughed at my mistake.

"Not here. I meant, these clothes are too bright. We need our blacks. Your place first, then the motel. Okay?"

"Okay."

My place was in darkness as Mum and Grant were visiting friends, so I didn't have to make any fake excuses about why I was changing into my stage blacks and going out again. I was glad Mum wasn't there to make any suggestions about black being an obvious colour to wear when you're out with a vampire, which she wouldn't have been able to resist doing. We managed to resist each other though – I grabbed my clothes and locked myself in the bathroom to change so Severn couldn't help me – because then we would have got side-tracked and never left the house. I finished off the outfit by tying my hair back in a ponytail and pulling on a black beanie – no point dressing in black to merge with the night when your yellow hair stands out like a beacon. I clipped my maglight and my pocket knife to my belt, just in case, and I was ready for whatever we were heading into.

Severn was on edge as we walked to his motel - his eyes

flickering left and right in hunting mode – but nothing followed us. Or, at least, if it did, we didn't see it. Instead, we reached the motel without incident and I stayed in the lounge while Severn changed his clothes. Temptation averted for the second time. But we didn't leave straight away. Severn took advantage of the empty rooms to search Aiden and the Rev's belongings, looking for the notes they had been writing to each other earlier. He had no luck but I found their remains in the kitchen – a pile of ashes in the bottom of a pot they had used in lieu of a fireplace to burn them. Sev's response when I showed him was an angry animal grunt of frustration.

"Where do we start to look for them?" I asked as we left the motel.

"You know? I'm not sure, but our best bet might be the centre of town. Let's start with the nightclub area."

"I wish they had left the car here, it's a long walk."

"Not when we jog." Severn laughed at my horrified gasp. "Only as far as the bus stop. Come on." He grabbed my hand so I could keep up, which I struggled to do, even though he wasn't using his vampire speed. When we reached the bus stop, I leant against the street light, gasping for breath, my heart racing, while Severn looked perfectly calm. It wasn't fair!

We rode the bus all the way to the central bus exchange then walked down Lichfield Street, blending easily with the partying groups heading towards the nightclubs on the Strip. Seven said that was their favourite hunting ground so it was a logical place to start looking for the Rev and Aiden. Again, by his rapid head movements, I could tell Severn had his hunting senses on full alert, listening to every sound as we walked, hugging the dark side of the street under the shop verandas.

Getting inside the nightclubs proved impossible. Usually, when the boys hunted, Severn dressed up in a flash Italian business suit so he looked old enough to get inside, but in our blacks and with me by his side, there was no way we were going to meet the dress code, let alone pass me off as old enough to get in, even if they believed Severn's fake driver's licence. I had to resort to asking the bouncers guarding the nightclubs' doors if the other two had been there. If it was only Aiden we were looking for, it would have been impossible. One average-sized male with brown, wavy hair looks pretty much like thousands of others, but the Reverend was distinctive. At the third place I asked about two men, one of them about my lack of height, with long hair tied back in a ponytail, we struck the jackpot.

Well, almost. They had been there, but they had already left.

"Which way did they go?" I asked and we set off in the direction the bouncer pointed.

We got the same reaction at the next nightclub along the Strip, although this time they had left with two women. Severn looked concerned when he heard the bouncer's description of them.

"That's what I was worried about," he said, without explaining what he meant. I wasn't letting him away with that, so I dragged him into the nearest café, bought us both a coffee and pushed him towards a corner table where we could talk.

"Talk!" I ordered.

"I could be wrong," he protested. "Those women might just have been their dinner."

"If you're wrong, then you're wrong, but at least tell me what you might be wrong about, in case you're right, because right doesn't sound like it's a good thing."

"You're not going to like it."

"I don't like not knowing what's going on, either. Stop making excuses and tell me who you think it is."

Severn tried to gain time by sipping his coffee slowly. I held mine but I didn't drink it. Instead, I glared at him until he gave in, put his coffee down and breathed heavily.

"The girls. Meredith and Olivia. I think it's the girls. I think they're here."

"That's impossible! Isn't it? Aren't they in France? With Finn? He wouldn't let them leave, surely?"

"That's what I keep telling myself, too, but who else could it be?"

"Millions of other people," I laughed. "Let's be sensible here. You've only seen the flash a couple of times. I've seen it a few times. But we haven't really seen anything. Neither of us has actually seen an identifiable person. It might have been a trick of the light, or your average east-side burglar going about his nightly breaking and entering. There's no reason to assume it's Meredith and Olivia, is there?"

"If it was just the whatever-it-is that's following us, I would agree with you, but there's Julia. Another body on a Brighton beach. That's what's got me worried. And I'll bet that's what Aiden and the Rev are panicking about too, because, if it is them, we've got a real problem. With no-one to keep them in check, those girls are dangerous and there will be more dead bodies before we catch them."

"But it sounds like Aiden and the Rev have caught them. If that bouncer is correct, they're all together right now, doing the rounds of the night clubs, snacking on the locals."

"I don't know if that's good or bad," Severn said, "because it kind of suggests they knew the girls were here."

"Unless they guessed before you did. No, think about it, if the girls had left France, then someone at the monastery would have sent a message to the Rev — he is the boss after all. He must know."

"And he will have told Aiden as soon as he heard," Severn agreed.

"What do we do now? We can't keep walking the streets all night in the vain hope we run into them. Well, you can but I can't. I'm getting cold and I need to get some sleep because the show starts again tomorrow. I know, back in the gardens, finding them seemed like a good idea but right now, I'm a bit over it. Can we go home?"

"Is that an invitation?"

"No, it's a request to drop me safely at my front door, which will then leave you free to go back on the hunt, and you can do that faster without me to slow you down. Plus, if you change into your fancy suit, you can get into the clubs if you need to, because you can't do that with me here either."

With a nod of his head to show he agreed, we finished our coffee and set off to find a homeward bus.

CHAPTER THIRTEEN

Mum and Grant were home but, although Grant was sitting in the lounge, I could hear Mum in their bedroom so I was able to avoid any conversation about my clothing. I slipped out of my blacks and into my pyjamas before I risked facing Mum's inevitable questions. On the theory that attack was the best form of defence, I got in first.

"How was your dinner party?" I asked, trying to sound as if it really interested me.

"Lovely," Mum answered. "Apart from the food. The food was terrible. Much as I enjoy their company, and she is one of my oldest friends, Janet cannot cook to save herself."

"We stopped for takeaways on the way home," Grant added. "Do you want a chip? They're still vaguely warm."

"Um, no thanks." Cold chips. Yum.

"But the conversation was good," Mum said. "Everyone was talking about that drone."

"What drone?" I asked.

"The one on the news," Grant said. "Haven't you seen it? It's amazing. It's huge, life-size. It looks like a demon. It's all over social media. Get on your computer and check it out."

"I will be interested to hear what you think it is," Mum said in a tone that made me instantly suspicious. Something flying, because that's what drones do, life-size and looking like a demon. That could be a disaster.

You guys are in big trouble. Pic Aiden flying going viral

Because that's who it was. Spreading all over social media. Thousand of hits. A fortunately grainy and unsteady video of a figure flying above the estuary. A human-shaped body held aloft by huge wings, leathery like a bats. It was too dark to see its face but I could tell it was Aiden. I hit send on my text to Severn, skimmed the comments on the post, and went back to join Mum and Grant who looked up expectantly as I walked through the door.

"It's amazing, isn't it?" Grant said, his face lit up with excitement. "Whoever made that is ridiculously talented. I've seen videos of drones before that are done up to look like those demon characters from movies, but that thing actually flaps its wings. How did they do that?"

"Or it's not a drone, it's a demon," Mum said. "That's what they were saying at dinner, anyway." She looked at me. "Grant was extolling the virtues of the drone maker and Phillip was arguing all the reasons it couldn't be a machine. He was adamant it had to be a real demon. Then it got into a religious discussion about whether demons were real or not, and went downhill from there."

"I saw that argument when I skipped through the comments on the post," I said. "It looks like the discussion is going three ways – it's either a drone, a demon or an angel."

"Surely, if it was an angel it would be all pure white, with feathery wings. Wouldn't it?" Grant said.

"Who says?" Mum replied. "Just because some medieval painters drew them all cutesy, doesn't mean to say they really are. In the bible, whenever one appears, they always start by saying 'fear not', which suggests they might look pretty scary."

"How do we know it isn't a fake?" I asked. "It could be just some good blue-screen video editing. It wouldn't be that hard to do if you had the equipment and the software."

"Don't spoil it." Grant pouted like a petulant child. "I want to believe it's a fabulous drone."

"Then you go on believing that," Mum said, patting his arm soothingly. "I think I will join the angel camp – until proven otherwise. Now let's get to bed, we've all got a show tomorrow."

I was happy to escape to my room where I sat on the edge of my bed waiting for the inevitable tap on the window. I didn't have to wait long.

Severn went straight to my computer and watched the video several times. He read through the comments before speaking.

"You're right. We've got big trouble. That's definitely Aiden."

"What are you going to do?"

"I don't know. I've got to find them first. All we can do at the moment is be grateful that it's such a lousy video and you can't see his face. It looks like the idiot was playing in the thermals, so he's flying fairly high up. Which is good. But we have to make sure he doesn't do it again because, sooner or later, someone's going to get a decent shot and then all hell will break loose."

"I would think that's going to happen as soon as the Rev sees this," I said.

"Hell, yes."

"Did you read the comments? Most people are like Grant and think he's a drone but the religious lot are divided. Are you angels or demons?"

"At least no-one has suggested vampires yet. I suppose we can be grateful for that."

"Should I add that? Just to stir the pot?"

"Don't you dare!" Severn sat back, took off his glasses and rubbed his eyes. "There are days when I wish I could walk away from all this. Aiden is an idiot and the girls, if they are in town, are a law unto themselves. If the three of them are together, I don't think the Rev is going to be able to control them. I'll go out and have another look for them, but if I can't find the Rev by tomorrow, I'll have no option. I'll have to call the monastery and get some help. I'm going to need Brother Martin the fix-it man."

"The Rev will be back. They both will. We've got a show tomorrow. They won't miss that – the Rev's too professional not to turn up, even if Aiden doesn't."

"You're right. There's no point in me traipsing all over town trying to find them. I've got a better idea. I'll bring the Rev to me."

Severn fiddled with my computer, pulled his phone out of his pocket and smiled when it pinged.

"That'll do it." He grinned at me. "I've emailed a copy of that video to him and to me, with a message to him that I will be at the motel waiting for his explanation. As I know he won't have an explanation, just a lot of angry questions, that should bring him running. I'll let you know what happens."

"And in the meantime, I'll let Mum know it isn't a demon or an angel, it's one of her friendly, resident vampires."

"Like that will surprise her. Not."

"Let's just hope that nobody starts linking the flying creature to the body on the beach and deciding that's why there were no footprints nearby," I said.

"Demon blamed for body drop. If that headline turns up in the morning paper, that's my cue to leave – but I bet Aiden would love it. I just hope the publicity doesn't encourage him to fly again but, knowing him, it probably will. He's probably going to work out where the video was taken from then fly over there on purpose."

"What happens to you guys if you break the rules about flying? Is there an official punishment? Do the elders clip your wings. Like budgies?"

Severn laughed at me. "Not a bad idea. No. There are no official rules except using common sense. It's all about survival – of the whole guild as well as each of us individually. We know we can't afford to be seen, that we have to be careful, and there is punishment for anyone who becomes a threat to the guild's survival. But it's a lot worse than having your wings clipped. Not that clipping our wings would be possible anyway – you can clip a bird's flight feathers but we haven't got feathers so that wouldn't work. I suppose you could cut big holes in them though, that would stop us getting airborne. I might suggest that to the Rev for Aiden."

"Or just take him back to France."

"If he's lucky."

I could tell by his narrowed eyes and the quiet snarl in his voice that the next meeting between him and Aiden could get nasty and I had no intention of fuelling his anger any higher, so I faked a yawn, wrapped my arms around him and gave him a kiss on his cheek.

"Go," I said with another kiss, "The Rev will have seen your email by now. He's probably back at the motel already. Go, meet him. Sort this mess out. Or, at least dump it on him so it isn't your problem. I'll see you tomorrow for the big reveal to Mum."

"Oh hell, I don't know what's worse."

But he kissed me goodnight anyway.

CHAPTER FOURTEEN

I woke to Aiden flying on breakfast television. Mum waved her hand in the direction of the kitchen, which I translated as telling me to pour my own coffee, then patted the couch beside her, all without turning her head away from the sight on the screen. As I joined her, the programme had moved back to the panel of presenters who were arguing the three options of drone, demon or angel. To add fuel to the suggestions, they cut back and forth between the presenters and reporters in different locations, all interviewing a different expert. We listened to a competitive drone pilot, a film-maker who specialised in animation and CGI who proclaimed the video was an elaborate and beautifully-made hoax, and the local archbishop who quoted ancient books describing angels and demons but ended up agreeing that it was probably a clever fake. Mum said nothing.

Once the programme had moved on to talk about rugby, I wandered off to the kitchen to make myself some toast and Mum, still not making any comments about the flying demon, went the other way, towards her bedroom. A few minutes later I heard the shower running, so I figured Mum wasn't in any hurry to get my course application started. Neither was I.

I took my time, munching toast and sipping coffee, until Mum reappeared, then had my own shower and dressed. Blue jeans, purple hoodie, and striped socks to keep my feet warm. Mum looked like an advertisement for summer in peach-coloured capris and matching top. Even her tiny, strapped sandals matched.

"You look very flash," I said. "Are you going somewhere?"

"No," Mum replied. "I just had a feeling it might be a good day to be prepared for anything."

"That sounds like one of your creepy witchy vibes," I said, not liking where this could be going.

"No, yes, maybe it is. Who knows. But, bring it on. Like I said, I am prepared for whatever comes my way."

"Like demons flying over Christchurch?" I teased.

"Them, too. Bring them on. But first, let's get this application of yours done."

Mum ushered me through to my bedroom where we turned on my computer and clicked onto the MAINZ website.

"I've spoken to Grant about this and he thinks it's a great idea," Mum said. "It's something you are obviously good at, and he's been around theatres long enough to know how sought-after good sound technicians are. We are right behind you, supporting this all the way."

"Thanks. Mum. That's really good to know. Oh look, we don't even have to print out the form – we can do it all online."

On the whole, the process was simple and logical and we worked our way through the questions methodically, until we reached the final click-to-submit button. I looked at Mum, she looked at me, we both smiled, nodded our heads and I clicked. Application submitted. We deserved a coffee, and maybe a chocolate biscuit. Severn must have smelled the coffee as he arrived just as we were pouring it.

"Good timing." Mum smiled as he entered. "Riley, grab another cup."

"I can do that," Severn said, reaching over my head to fetch a mug from the cupboard behind me, then giving me a quick kiss as he stepped back again.

"Did you find Aiden and the Rev?" I asked.

"Did you lose them?" Mum asked in her innocently stirring voice.

"Yes to both," Severn answered, giving Mum one of his sweetest smiles. Inwardly, I cringed. If they were both going to spend the morning in a smiley-face stand-off, Grant could find us all smothered to death by sarcasm when he got home from work. We were heading towards the cliff edge of this game of 'I know you know' that Mum had been playing with us and it was time to jump off the edge into the abyss. The only question was who was going to jump first, or would Mum push us over.

"The Rev arrived just after I got back to the motel," Severn continued. "Aiden came back quite a bit later."

I could tell by his tone of voice that there was a much larger story in that, but it would have to wait. There was no way I was going to ask for details in front of Mum and I could see by his tightened lips that there was no way Severn was offering any.

"Did you find out where they had been?" was the only question I dared to ask.

"Yeah, some club called the Heads of Cerberus. It's in a cellar down a back alley, not on the main Strip, which is why I didn't find it earlier."

"I'm surprised the Reverend gets past the bouncers to get into a club," Mum said.

"Me too," Severn agreed. "Money talks."

"I've done my application," I said, changing the subject to something safer.

"Nice," Severn said. "I will remind the Rev to send them a reference for you. He knows the tutors so his word should be worth something."

"As long as it doesn't say Riley panics when faced with a challenge, bottles out and calls her boyfriend," I said.

"Never. It's more like to say Riley faces challenges head on and has gained a lot of experience in difficult live performance situations."

"Oh shucks." I faked a bad southern American accent.

Then Mum, who had been suspiciously quiet, hit us with the low blow.

"Have you seen the flying demon video, Severn? Have you got any ideas about what it could possibly be?"

Severn could have done several things. He could have pretended he hadn't seen it, feigned complete ignorance and asked what she was talking about. He could have agreed he had seen it and claimed it was definitely a fake. He could even have got into a discussion about demons. But, like a true vampire, he went straight for the jugular.

"No possibly about it. I know exactly what it is. It's worst case scenario trouble." He paused, drew breath and looked straight at Mum. "It's Aiden."

"Nice reply. Good joke," Mum said. "Although I suppose, if it was Aiden, it would solve the argument about demon or angel – I don't see Aiden wearing white or playing a harp."

"I wasn't joking. I mean it. It's Aiden."

He said it with such quiet determination that Mum stopped in the middle of forming her next comment, her mouth hanging open as she took in Severn's words.

"What are you telling me?" she finally gasped.

"Look, I think we should all sit down," Severn said. "Let's go into the lounge."

I guided Mum to her favourite armchair and joined Severn on the couch.

"We, Riley and I, talked about this yesterday," he said, his voice low and quiet. "We've both noticed the vibe lately and we thought today might be the ideal time to call your bluff, to come clean. But it wasn't supposed to be quite like this. Aiden has thrown a real spanner in the works. So," he paused and drew a long breath, giving Mum a gap to jump in.

"Call my bluff?" she asked. "About what?"

"Lost Boys," I said. "All the damn vampires."

"Oh, come on, you two." Mum laughed at us. "What is this all about? It's only January, it's not April Fools Day. Why are you pranking me? Okay, I admit I have been giving you a hard time, making a few bad vampire jokes, but come on, it's just because you guys are so vampire-like. But no matter what I've implied about you, I am not going to believe that drone flying thing was Aiden. That's ridiculous. Anyway, vampires don't fly – they would have to turn back into bats to do that, wouldn't they?"

"No, we don't," Severn said. "We have wings. Mrs Watson, you might have been making jokes but both Riley and I know that's because, somehow, you've suspected the truth for quite a while. Those jokes were your way of letting us know that you know, weren't they?"

"Call me Susan and yes, yes they were. Well, I knew, or I thought I knew, but I didn't really know because I've only heard Grandma's stories about when she met a vampire and she could have been making it up to scare me, even though he didn't sound very scary."

"Great-Grandma met a vampire?" I asked before Severn could frame the same question. "When? Where?"

"At her house, in Dunedin, not long before I was born, I think."

"Great-Grandma, the witchy one?" I asked. I looked at Severn who was trying to work out Mum's age and doing the maths in his head. If it was forty years, give or take a year, since the body on Dunedin's Brighton beach and that wasn't long before Mum was born, how old was she now and could the vampire have been one of them?

"This is getting crazy." Severn put his hands to his lowered forehead and shook his head before he looked at Mum again. "How, why, did your grandmother have a vampire in her house and why did he tell her he was one?"

"The same reason you're in my house now," Mum replied. "Grandma met him backstage in a theatre. Riley, you know that's who I got my singing voice from. Grandma was always in the local shows. But like you also said, Grandma was a witchy woman. She told me she knew they were vampires before he told her. She said they smelled like vampires. That's how I picked you guys. Grandma said vampires had a distinctive, soft, musky scent like leather, which we noticed about you lot. All the wardrobe ladies were taking bets on what aftershave you used. They loved it."

"It's probably the wings," Severn said.

"Seriously?" Mum almost snorted. "You're really going with the wing story? You haven't even proved you're vampires yet. Where are your fangs?"

"You asked for it." Severn stood, turned his back on us, took off his glasses and hung his head. Then with a deep breath and a slight shake of his body, he straightened up, threw back his head and spun back to us in full hunting mode, his eyes flashing ultra-bright blue, his fangs extended. Mum gasped, pressing herself back into her chair in involuntary fear.

"Wow!" she said as Severn pulled himself back to normal and replaced his glasses. "Wow!"

"Wait, there's more," Severn said with a smile that wasn't totally reassuring. "Riley, can you please rescue those ornaments from that shelf over there? I don't want to break them and this room isn't very big."

Mum looked surprised at the comment as she was proud of her large lounge but I knew what was coming. Severn waited for me to move the ornaments then, with a deft tug, pulled off his t-shirt. Moving to the centre of the room, he flexed his shoulders and slowly unfurled his wings until they touched the opposite walls.

"Oh my god," was all Mum could say. "Oh my god!"

CHAPTER FIFTEEN

"I have a thousand questions," Mum said as Severn furled his wings and put his t-shirt back on. He had spread his wings almost to their full span and he had even let Mum touch them, eliciting gasps of "they're so soft" as she stroked them like he was a cat. Knowing how Severn hated anyone touching them, I was impressed how patient he was as Mum looked at them from every direction and I could see the relief on his face when she finally let him furl them up.

"I'll bet you do," I said in response to her question. "More coffee first?"

"Yes, please," they both said in unison.

As we boiled the jug and spooned instant coffee into our mugs, Mum couldn't stop staring at Severn. I wasn't sure if that was good or bad. I was hoping for good as the small smiles seemed to outweigh the furrowed scowls. Coffee made and a new packet of chocolate biscuits opened, we pulled out chairs and settled around the dining table where we passed the biscuits between us.

"Fire away," Severn offered. "Ask any questions you like."

"How old are you really?" Mum asked.

"A hundred and twenty nine. I'm the youngest. The Rev is seven hundred plus."

"Wow," Mum said. "Where are you from? None of you have recognisable accents. You all speak very correctly, like you've had elocution lessons."

"We have. We've all tried to lose our original accents. It's part of being able to blend in without being noticed. I'm from Scotland originally, the Rev is French and Aiden is English from near the Welsh border."

"Is that why you went back to France? Do you all live at the Reverend's house?"

"His monastery, yes."

"His monastery?" Mum spluttered into her coffee.

"Yep, the monastery of Montagne des Anges – the Mountain of Angels. Note that – angels, not demons. Our locals wouldn't appreciate you calling us demons."

"They think you're angels? They know you can fly?"

"Well, not quite. For centuries they've seen angels flying over the monastery. They've just never connected the angels directly with the unassuming monks in their long, woollen robes. They just think we are extremely pious and, therefore, blessed to be visited by heavenly creatures."

"If you're really a monk, how come you're going out with my daughter? Aren't you supposed to be celibate?"

"Mum!"

"Sorry, dear, but he did say I could ask anything."

"I'm not a monk," Severn said. "David is. That's why we call him the Reverend. I just live there. About thirty of the residents are actually monks, the rest of us fake it, but it's okay because it's damned cold there and the robes are warm. All of us are vampires."

"Next question. When Riley finishes her course and goes off touring with your crew, will she have to become a vampire too?"

"Only if she wants to. No pressure, Not essential. I guarantee it."

"But you have bitten her, haven't you?"

"Um..." Severn hesitated and looked at me.

"Yes, he has," I said. "I asked him too. He's ethical, Mum, last time I asked him to bite me, he refused. We're careful, Mum. It's all right. He's not going to drink so much that I die and it's not going to turn me into a vampire – that's a whole different process. Hey, look on the bright side, I can't get pregnant like Anita did."

"Oh, I can just see myself explaining that to the ladies in the wardrobe department. My daughter's boyfriend drinks her blood but she won't get pregnant. This is too weird."

"Sorry." Severn looked chastised but Mum laughed at him.

"Cheer up. Like I said, like you guessed, I'm not completely shocked and I'm certainly not horrified. I've known you too long now to be frightened of you."

"Can I ask you a question," Severn asked. "In Dunedin, when your grandmother told you about that vampire, did she say what he looked like?"

Mum thought hard before she answered.

"Like you would expect a vampire to look. My memory's pretty vague but I remember her saying he was rather gorgeous - tall, dark, handsome. Black hair, black clothes. Classic B-grade movie vampire. But I never met him, and I was only little when she told me, so my memory could be completely wrong."

"Did she tell you his name?"

"No, sorry, I don't remember. I'm not sure I ever heard it. Why? Oh, you're wondering if you know him, aren't you?"

"I'm wondering if it was Seth Borman," Severn replied. "The timing fits. We were in Dunedin then and Seth was often going off doing his own thing without telling us."

"Seth?" Mum stood up and paced the kitchen to help her memory. "The gorgeous hunk of flyman, Seth? Could have been. Tall, dark, handsome, yep, it could well have been Seth. Speaking of him, what's he doing now? He has a few questions to answer about poor Julia, from what I hear."

"Like what?" Severn sounded like he dreaded hearing the answer.

"From what I hear, he was going out with Julia during the show and then dumped her. I know you left early, and Seth wasn't seen after that night, so I presume he left with you, but he could have had the decency to say something to Julia before he left. Just walking out was pretty rude."

Severn glanced sideways at me and I knew he was about to tell Mum more truths than we had ever intended.

"He didn't speak to her because he couldn't," Severn said quietly. "He was dead. He travelled back to France with me in a body bag."

"Oh! Can I ask what happened?"

"It's better if you don't know. It was between us vampires. Things got complicated and very messy. But it's a pity we didn't know about Julia. He kept that very quiet. If we had known, I'm sure the Rev would have made up a story to cover him leaving that she would have believed."

"What about the rest of the crew that was with you before? The older guy and the two girls? Are they all vampires too?"

"Yes they are. Finn really is Aiden and Meredith's father and Meredith really is Aiden's twin sister. Finn is loving it at the monastery. He spends his days pottering around fixing things, like the plumbing, and wiring new electrical fittings, so the monastery loves him too. Meredith and Olivia are supposed to be at the monastery too, under supervision, which translates as being deprogrammed from Seth's bad habits, but I have a horrible feeling they might not be."

"We think they're here," I added. "We think they've been

following us around."

"And now that Aiden's been stupid enough to be seen flying," Severn said. "we are smack in the middle of vampire hell."

"What did the Rev say when you showed him the video?" I asked.

Severn grinned. "I can't quote him exactly but it was a long sentence full of ancient French curse words."

"He wasn't impressed?"

"What do you think? He was all for tracking Aiden down straight away and dealing to him on the spot. I managed to calm him down and not to tackle Aiden as soon as he got back, but they will both wake up soon, so I should get back and referee the discussion that's bound to happen."

"Should I come with you?" I asked.

"No, leave it to me. I'll see you at the show later this afternoon. I'm not guaranteeing the others will be there too, but we can manage if they don't turn up." He turned to Mum. "Thank you for taking this so well. I couldn't believe it when Riley found out and wasn't scared of me, or shocked, or repulsed, but I can see where she gets it from. You two are unreal."

Mum watched as I walked Severn to the door and kissed him goodbye, then she laughed.

"I'll notch that one up, I've just been called unreal by an undead."

She walked away, singing the verse by Tom Petty about the vampires walking through the valley. I hoped she would run out of vampire songs soon.

CHAPTER SIXTEEN

I figured it wouldn't take Mum long to swing into her usual remedy for when she had too many things to think about and I was right. After Severn left, she went into a frenzy of house cleaning, which I dodged by retreating to my room. About an hour later she knocked on my door with the question I was expecting.

"I am still reeling from this morning's information overload. My head is spinning and I need a break. Do you want to come shopping?

"Yeah, okay. Where are we going?"

"Northlands."

"Awesome. If we're going there, can I text Anita and see if she wants to meet us?"

"Better than that. If she wants to come, we'll pick her up on the way."

I flicked Anita a text and twenty minutes later the three of us were walking through the mall entrance. I knew from experience that Mum would head straight for the clothing shops where she would spend ages in the fitting rooms, trying things on, so it was good to have Anita to talk to while I stood, endlessly waiting with the occasional nodding of approval at Mum's choices. Anita had seen the video too.

"What about that drone?" she said, almost jumping with excitement. "Isn't it the coolest thing ever? Caleb must have watched the video about a thousand times, trying to work out how it's done."

"I saw it on telly this morning," I said, playing it down. "It's cool if it's real, but I reckon it's just some clever animation."

"Don't spoil the magic!"

"Why not? I'm backstage crew. We're the guys who know the truth behind all the magic. We're the cynical, unshockable realists who work behind the curtains creating it. So I'm in the camp that says it's a fake, sorry."

"Well that's boring," Anita sulked, but not for long. "You should see my costume, it's amazing."

"Costume? You've lost me. What costume?"

"For the MFR. Remember I told you how Caleb's family are all into medieval re-enactment and they were going to take me to the next event?

"Oh yeah. You said you were going as someone posh and Caleb's mum was helping you make your outfit. So what's it like?"

"A-maze-ing! It's some kind of super-soft velvet with braid trim around the neck and a silver cord under the bust. I'm supposed to be from the twelfth century, so it's got these absolutely humungous sleeves that fall in these huge points right down to the ground. I'll have to practise wearing it so I don't trip over them."

"What does Caleb wear? A codpiece?"

"No way! His persona is a wandering minstrel so he's just got a tunic over leggings. And, yes, before you ask, it does cover his bum. I'm looking forward to it, it sounds like so much fun."

"I'm just glad you two have found something you can enjoy doing together, and with baby when it arrives."

"Me, too." Anita nodded enthusiastically. "It's so weird. I hardly noticed him at school and now I find we are so alike, its spooky. What about you and Severn? Do you like the same things?"

"Yes and no." Let me think – he drinks blood, I let him. Not a good answer. "We both enjoy being backstage crew and we're working well together on this show. He really knows his stuff behind the sound desk, that's for sure. I've got a lot to learn to keep up with him. Which is why I'm doing the sound engineering course. I want to be his equal backstage, not his bumbling apprentice. But there are other ways we are not at all alike." He's undead, I'm alive. "He's way more into computers that I am, but that's okay, I can do other things when he's being a geek. We like the same type of chocolate, so that's got to be a good sign."

"I can think of nothing more important," Anita said with an expansive wave of her hands that ended in her pointing towards the fitting room. "Hey, your mum is waving at us. I think we're needed."

We hurried over to Mum who had started to panic as she had noticed the time.

"Look at me," she moaned, "I've done it again. I got so carried away trying on these outfits, I've taken up all our shopping time. You girls must be so bored."

"We're fine," I assured her. "We've been swapping gossip. But, if we're going to eat before we go to Mona Vale, you do need to make some decisions. How many of these dresses are you going to buy?"

Mum picked a dress off the rack and handed it to me. "This one," she said, "and this one." She handed me a second dress, then a third. "And I can't possibly leave this one. Do I need that one with the stripe? No, no, some self control needed here. Just these three. Let's go."

Credit card processed and parcel wrapped, Mum swept us off down the mall, telling herself off every time she slowed to browse in a clothes shop window, but encouraging us to wander through the shops that we liked which, for Anita, included any shop that had fluffy toys. It was in one of these shops, while Anita was cooing over a bright blue bear, that Mum found the bat.

"Riley, look," she said, pulling it out of the rack. "I have to get this for Severn."

"Seriously?"

"No, that's the whole point, it's not serious at all. Look, it's just right. It's got this little, black body then look, you undo this Velcro and its wings unfurl. It's perfect. He'll get the joke."

I had to laugh. It was Mum's way of saying she accepted Severn, as my boyfriend, as a vampire, as a family member. My mum was, as Severn said, unreal.

Mum bought the bat and treated Anita to the blue bear as well, then checked her watch and declared it was time to leave. We dropped Anita and her bear outside her house and drove home, arriving half an hour before Grant. As his car pulled into the drive, Mum grabbed my arm.

"Let's not tell Grant anything about today." Mum dropped her voice to a conspiratorial whisper. "We can say Severn came over and we can tell him you put your application in, but nothing else. Okay?"

"Whatever else are you talking about, Mum?" I batted my eyelids and put on my innocent face. "Your shopping trip?"

"You know what I mean."

"Of course I do. Mum, I've known about Severn for months and I haven't said anything. I'm not exactly going to drop vampires into the dinner conversation. Just make sure you don't."

"I won't. And we need to be on the same page if he brings up that damned video. Let's agree with him that it's a drone."

"No. If we agree with him, he'll automatically be suspicious. We will agree that it's okay for him to think it's a drone but I'll say I think it's a fake – that's what I told Anita so I'd better be consistent – and you say you bow to his opinion that it's probably a drone but you are secretly hoping it's a demon. Okay?"

"Okay."

Mum scuttled back to the lounge and by the time Grant had parked his car and come inside, she was posed in her armchair as if she had been there for hours. Good acting. As he came into the room she faked a surprised look.

"Is that the time already or are you home early? Sit down and put your feet up, I'll get you a beer and make us all some sandwiches so we can eat before we go to the show."

"Thanks, love," Grant said, "but coffee instead of beer, please. I'll save the beer until after the show. I'd hate to have it go to my head and make me forget my lines, or fall over my sword."

"You wouldn't be the first actor to do that," Mum said. "How was your day?"

"Drone overload. All day. Nobody could talk about anything else. If one more person mentions that damned video I swear I will go postal!"

Mum swivelled in her chair and grinned at me. I gave her a thumbs-up sign. One conversation avoided.

CHAPTER SEVENTEEN

We couldn't avoid the video at Mona Vale. Everyone was talking about it. Except us. We kept our heads down and pretended we were too busy running cables and hanging speakers to get into any discussions. Aiden was especially quiet.

I had fully expected him not to turn up at all, but he was in the driving seat when they pulled up. As I walked over to join them, I could see the Rev talking and Aiden hanging his head and when he got out of the car he was definitely not his usual ebullient self. I thought I had better warn them what to expect.

"Everyone is talking about the video," I said. "So far it's an even split between animated fake and a drone, although at least three of them are voting for demon and wearing crucifixes around their necks."

"Oh shit," Aiden said. He looked down and scuffed the ground with his boot, looking so dejected I actually felt sorry for him.

"At least nobody knows the truth," I said.

"And we're going to make sure we keep it that way, aren't we, Aiden?" The Rev's tone suggesting he had already laid down some ground rules for expected vampire behaviour.

I could see Aiden wanted to reply, but he bit his words back. "Let's just get this done," he said. "And don't worry, I'm just going to shut up and do my job." He looked up and shook his finger at us. "Same goes for you lot – just don't talk about it."

"I agree with that," the Rev said as Aiden walked away. "Let's all be too busy to talk. Don't take part in any conversations about that damned video. The less it's talked about, the sooner it will be forgotten. We will talk about it – together – after the show and in private. There are things you should know."

"Things?" Severn asked, his head cocked to one side, one eyebrow raised quizzically over his glasses. "I suppose you could call Meredith and Olivia things. They mightn't like it though."

The Reverend looked at Severn in genuine surprise. Severn just tucked his head to the other side and curled his lips in a knowing smirk.

"Later!" the Rev glared at him. "We will discuss this later."

"Yes, boss, anything you say, boss." Severn flicked a facetious salute, grabbed my hand and followed Aiden, leaving the Rev standing, glaring at our departing backs.

"Not a happy camp?" I asked.

"Happy? No. Volatile, simmering, volcanic are more the words I would use. But, I will give him this, Aiden is genuinely shocked he got caught on camera. You have to remember, he's older than photography. It was invented about fifty years before I was born but Aiden's a lot older than me. In his head, photographs are still bits of paper developed in fluid – he might have the latest cell phone in his pocket but he hasn't really got his head around the speed technology has developed in the last ten years or so. It had honestly never occurred to him that someone would see him flying and capture that on their phone. The last few hours have been a big learning curve for him."

"Yeah, he looked pretty ashamed. I've never seen him so meek and quiet."

"Me neither. I missed the blow-out. If they did have a shouting match, it was over by the time I caught up with them. By then, they had simmered down to that angry-Rev, sulking-Aiden situation you just witnessed. But I know Aiden too well. There's no way he didn't give as good as he got at one stage in the proceedings."

"What's the story with Meredith and Olivia? Are they part of what's going on? The Rev didn't seem to happy that you knew about them being here."

"Yeah, that was a bit of a shock to him, wasn't it?" Severn gave me a wicked little grin. "I guess tonight's discussion could get interesting."

"I hate it when you use that word."

"What word?"

"Interesting. Around you, interesting always equals trouble."

"Interesting you should say that." Another evil grin. "Watch this space. Now let's get this show on the road, shall we? You're on radio mics."

For the next hour we kept our heads down, ran cables, set up speakers and avoided any attempts to draw us into conversations about the video. The Rev worked alongside Severn and me, setting up the sound desk, but Aiden made himself scarce by scuttling up the lighting tower to help Cameron and Danny. He didn't come back to us until the stage manager had called "beginners" and we were seated behind the desk, headphones on and chocolate resting on the script in front of us. I was doing a final paranoid piffel check of the radio mics when Aiden appeared beside me. For a moment I ignored him to ask Severn a question.

"Why do you call that piffling? That's the sort of thing I should know before I start my course. I don't want to look like an idiot."

Severn laughed at me. "Piffel. P.F.L. Pre-fade listen. You are hearing the sound on that channel before you fade it up to go through the speakers. When that button is pushed, you can hear it through your headphones but no-one else can. Watch it, your chocolate is disappearing."

I looked sideways just in time to see Aiden's hand retreating with half my chocolate bar clutched tightly in its fingers. I slapped my hand out to grab the rest of my bar.

"No!" I held the remains protectively against my chest. "Mine!"

Aiden just laughed and jumped off the scaffolding tower, holding the stolen chocolate aloft as he ran away.

"He's back to normal," I said,

"Damn," Severn answered, then spoke into his headset microphone. "Sound standing by."

He nodded at me. I adjusted my headset and poised my hand over the faders for the musicians, listening for the stage manager's call and watching the band's conductor who had lifted his baton. I was finally getting the hang of the timing. The conductor lifted his baton, the musicians straightened in their seats, their instruments ready, and I slid the faders up the sound desk. The conductor brought his baton down, the music rushed through the speakers and the show began. I remembered to breathe.

"Nice." Severn gave me a thumbs-up, his ears tuned to his own headset for the next cue which would be his to bring up the radio microphone for the first actor to hit the stage. I faded the musicians down as the overture ended and popped some of my remaining chocolate in my mouth.

It wasn't until we stopped for interval and she came running up to the tower that I remembered Anita was coming to the show with Caleb and his parents.

"Show me what you do," she said, clambering up the side of the tower to stand beside my chair. She looked at the two side-by-side sound desks – the bigger one under Severn's control and the smaller one that I controlled the musicians from. "Wow! So many slidey-thingies. How do you know which ones to push up and down?"

"Who says we do?" Severn smiled over at her. "Maybe we just push them at random."

"I'm not that gullible," Anita replied. "It was a serious question."

"They're all labelled," I explained. "See? These sticky labels say what mic is which and the notes on my script," I pointed to a page, " tell me which one is needed when. The stage manager is telling me in advance, too."

"Where does he sit?"

"Beside the stage."

"So how can hear him?"

"It's a her, not a him, and through these," I patted my headset. "We can talk to each other. In fact, all the technical crew can talk to each other. Cameron up there on the top of the lighting tower can hear us too."

To prove the point, Cameron waved at us.

"So you can't gossip about anyone or say anything rude?" Anita said, waving back.

"The lighting guys tell rude jokes all the time," I said, "and we all swear at actors who do stupid things."

"And musicians. We swear a lot at musicians," Severn added. "But, yeah, we do have to remember that others can hear us, and remember that they're trying to work and not miss their cues. We also have to remember that we are not backstage – we're sitting out the front of the stage, at the back of the audience, so we can't interrupt their enjoyment of the show. People don't pay to hear the sound guy's voice ruining their show with dumb jokes."

"I am impressed. All this," Anita swept her arm over the desk. "It's all so cool. I always thought what you did backstage must be really boring – all in black and in the dark – but it looks really fun. And interesting."

"We're not allowed to say 'interesting' around Riley," Severn said as he stood up and stretched his muscles.

"Why not?" Anita asked.

"Because Riley says interesting always equals trouble, so she's banned the word."

"I have not," I said. "It only equals trouble when you say it. Anita can use the word, she's safe. You can't. Well, you can but I will treat it with deep suspicion. Anyway, can we get off this tower. I need to move. Where's Caleb? Let's go say hello."

"Sorry," Severn reached out to stop me climbing down the scaffolding. "You can't run away. We'll be on standby again in a few minutes and we need to make sure the radio mic changes have happened."

I was just about to apologise for forgetting my job and dash off to the dressing room tent when Aiden jogged up.

"Done," he said, in answer to Severn's comment that, of course, he had heard. "But I've just come to tell you to keep an ear on mic three. It was flashing red so I changed the batteries but they were fresh before the show, so either they were faulty or there's a problem with the pack itself. Let me know if it cuts out and I'll switch it for mic twelve."

"Okay, thanks," Severn said, leaning over to his script and flicking through a few pages. "She's only on for a short scene, then she's off until nearer the end so check it when she comes off and let me know how it's holding out. Good spotting."

"Is it worth chocolate?" Aiden gave me his best hopeful puppy look. I was torn between rewarding him for doing what was, actually, my job and wanting all the rest of my stash for myself so I felt mean but relieved when Severn pulled yet another block from one of the copious pockets of his coat.

"My shout," he said, handing the block to Aiden. "It's all yours."

For the first time since we arrived at Mona Vale, I saw Aiden light up, a wide smile spreading across his face, flashing white teeth with just a hint of sharp fang.

"Thanks, mate," he said in a bad attempt at a Kiwi accent. "I needed that."

"You're welcome," Severn smiled back. "Now head off backstage because our comms just flashed, so we need to be back at our stations. Sorry, Anita, you need to climb down – the show's about to start again."

CHAPTER EIGHTEEN

The night was falling as the show ended to rapturous applause and the actors raced out front to greet their families and friends. Severn said he would coil the cables for me but I hadn't been on the ball at interval so I couldn't let them do my job again. I was unplugging a speaker and flicking the cable into a neat coil when Anita found me.

"I am a converted fan of live theatre," she gushed. "That was so good. Your step-dad can act, can't he? He was funny. And you and Severn. You look like professionals, all in your black clothes and so organised. I didn't realise what you did was so important."

"Severn looks like a professional because he is one," I said. "And I will be soon."

"Who was the other guy — the one who came for chocolate?"

"That's Aiden. He's a professional too. Same crew as Severn. They travel together and at the end of the year, that will be me too."

"How long does it take to clear this up?" Anita asked. "Can you sneak off and come with us?"

"No, sorry, I'll be ages. It takes a while to pack all this up."

"If you've got another show tomorrow, why can't you just leave it set up?"

"Because it's outside. If we were in a theatre, it would have been set up a week before the show and stay in place until the show ended but here, outside, it's too risky. It would cost the company too much to have security on site every night, so we spend an hour or so before and after each show setting it up and breaking it down again."

"That sucks."

"Yep, it can suck, it's hard work, but it's good training for me. I've learnt heaps about what can, and will, go wrong, and how to fix it on the fly while the show is happening. I couldn't have done this without Severn, though. If he and the others hadn't flown to my rescue I would have folded in a screaming heap before rehearsals finished."

"He's pretty confident, isn't he?"

"He is now, yes. He wasn't when I first met him. There were a couple of others in the crew who bullied him, but he finally stood up to them and put them in their place." Yes he did – Seth's place was totally dead and Severn put him there. "Plus, on this show, they came to help me specifically with the sound, and that's Severn's area of expertise - the other two are lighting and set – so, although the Rev is technically the boss of the crew, Severn's in control when we're behind that desk."

"But they're not much older than we are – how come they know so much?"

I hate those questions. "They started young," I said, hoping I sounded convincing. I needed to change the subject, or get rid of her quickly. "Sorry I can't come with you, but I really need to get these cables packed up." I started coiling the cable again to give her a subtle hint.

"Okay, have fun." Anita took the hint. "I'll text you later."

With Anita gone, I worked faster, coiling the rest of the cables and delivering them to the container to be locked away. On my way I passed Aiden, nonchalantly carrying a giant speaker in each hand. I had tried to carry one on the first day and couldn't lift it, and he was carrying two as if they were bags of bread. Vampires!

"Hey, Riley," he called out. "Can you go back to the women's dressing room and get the box of radio mics please? I haven't had time to collect them."

"Sure, no problem. I'll just dump these first."

Which is why I saw the shadow.

I handed the cables to Severn at the container then sprinted around the back of the makeshift stage to reach the small bridge that would take me across the creek to the dressing room tents. I had my head down as I crossed the slippery bridge and as I looked up again, I saw a movement behind a large grove of trees. I stopped, stared straight at the spot and put my hands on my hips.

"Bring it on, bitch," I said, almost under my breath. I was tempted to yell it, but if it was Meredith or Olivia, I didn't have to shout. They would've heard me. I stood and watched, daring it to show itself, but nothing moved. After a significant pause, I gave the trees a two-fingered salute and continued on my way to collect the microphones, which I found neatly packed into their carry box. Mum would have done that. I grabbed the box and ran, not looking back at the grove of trees in case the shadow was still there.

I was puffing by the time I reached the container. I handed the box of microphones to Severn who tucked them in with the rest of our gear, then I leant against the container to get my breath back. I risked a glance back towards the stage, trying to make my movements look casual and unplanned, but it was getting too dark to see the stage, let alone the trees behind it. I had a quick debate with myself – do I tell Severn, or not? I decided on not. If I told him, he would tell the others and they would all rush off to look and, to be honest, I was tired and getting cold and I just wanted to leave. So I said nothing. Instead, I helped pack the last of the items away, watched Danny close the padlocks to secure the container door, and walked to the car. If Meredith was hiding out there in the dark, watching us, I hope she was entertained. No, actually, I hoped she was bored witless and freezing cold. I never did like her very much.

Severn caught up with me when I was halfway across the car park.

"Your mother has a very weird sense of humour. She gave me this." He pulled the toy bat out of his pocket to show me.

"Oh yes, weird is the word. I apologise for my mother. She spotted it in a toy shop and couldn't resist. Sorry about that."

"Don't apologise. I think it's funny." He held the bat up to his face and peered at its oversized eyes. "He's kinda cute."

"You're as weird as she is. Mum liked the way his wings unfurl then fold up again. She thought you would get the joke."

"I will find a suitable gift in return," Severn said, although the stress he put on the word 'suitable' made me think a game of one-upmanship may have just begun. The bat might only be round one of an escalating contest. Severn tucked the bat back into his coat pocket and gave me a smile that looked far too pleasant. Mum was in trouble.

We waited at the car for Aiden and the Rev to arrive with the keys, chatting with Cameron who tried and failed to tempt us into joining him on a junk food run. The talk of food made me hungry, though, so I convinced Aiden to take us through a drive-through when we got to our side of town. Back at the motel I tucked myself into a corner of the couch and stuffed myself with a burger and chips while I waited for the Reverend's important talk to begin. Severn tossed his coat, with bat in pocket, over the arm of the couch and joined me.

"Now the real show is about to begin," he said, sitting back and crossing his arms. I caught a glint of brightness in his eyes – his hunting mode was primed but he was keeping a lid on it. He was ready for a fight.

The Reverend took his time. He was last out of the car, last through the door, last to discard his coat and walk back to the lounge where he took his time, saying nothing until he had our undivided attention. Then he rocked slightly on his heels and spoke.

"Severn, Riley, I gather you two have figured out what Aiden and I have known for a couple of days. The girls are in town. Which means we need a containment plan."

"And the first part of your plan was to keep it hidden from us?" Severn snarled. "You and Aiden were going to sort them out by yourselves?"

"No, not at all, but we did want to be sure of our facts first. Now we are, so now we make a plan. Let's start with what we know."

"They're hanging out at the Heads of Cerberus nightclub, snacking as they see fit in their usual careless manner," Severn said. "Am I right?"

"What are they doing here?" I asked. "What do they want?" A thought came to me. "Even if they are here, why does it matter? Okay, at least one of them has been following Severn and me around, and someone was hiding in the trees after the show tonight, but why can't we just ignore them?"

"Because uncontrolled, they could blow our cover. They are messy hunters and leave evidence," the Reverend explained.

I shook my head to disagree. "You're not thinking straight. Yes, that might apply if you lot were together but right now, you're here and they are wherever they are hiding out. Even if they got caught being vampires, there's nothing to connect them to you three. If they jump the wrong guy in a back alley, if they become the scandal of the week, even if their wings and fangs make headline news like Aiden did, nobody is going to connect them with three teenagers, because that's what you look like, doing some amateur theatre."

The Rev opened his mouth to interrupt but I was in full flight. "I mean, honestly, nobody going to the show even notices us. Crew are invisible. I doubt anyone could pick you out from Cameron in a line-up. Sorry, guys, but I think you all need to take a chill pill. Leave the girls alone, finish the show, go back to France and let them do whatever they are here to do. Maybe they just wanted to go clubbing – I bet they can't do a lot of that in the monastery."

"I wish it was that simple." The Rev gained some time to compose his words by pulling the band out of his ponytail and tying it up again. "Believe me, ignoring them is very tempting, but if we do that, they will kill someone else. There will be another body on the beach. It will be on the same beach, probably in exactly the same spot, because that's Meredith's signature move. As the Grand Master of the Guild, I can't let that happen. Severn can walk away and say it's not his problem and I wouldn't blame him. Aiden can walk away but he won't because Meredith is his twin sister and he cares about her, but I can't walk away because, ultimately, she's my responsibility. I can't let her kill again."

CHAPTER NINETEEN

"I want to know what Aiden's going to do?" I said. "And you still haven't answered the question of how they got here when they were supposed to be under supervision in the monastery."

From the armchair he was curled up in, Aiden laughed. "Like that was ever going to work. They just waited until no-one was looking, climbed the stairs to the roof and flew away."

"And flew all the way across to the other side of the world? On their own wings?" I said as sarcastically as I could.

"How about to the nearest town with a train station," Aiden replied, matching my tone. "They did take a bag, with clothes and passports. We're pretty strong – we can carry a bag and fly at the same time."

"Passports?" The Rev exploded. "How the hell did they get their passports? We confiscated them."

"Same way we got ours. They went down to the printing press and made new ones."

"Merde! Putain! Ca me fait chier!" The Rev was so angry he had reverted to French curses.

I looked at Severn for a translation. He winked at me and grinned. "Let's just say he's a tad miffed."

"Aiden," I persisted. "You must know more than you are telling us. It might be news to us that they're here, but I really don't believe it was news to you. Meredith isn't just your sister, she's your twin, and if turning into a vampire heightens your senses, I bet it's heightened your twin-thing communication as well. I reckon you both know exactly where the other one is, all the time." I glared at him, daring him to deny it.

"You have been going off on your own in the middle of the night," the Rev said.

"To meet them?" Severn asked.

"So what?" Aiden retorted. "Yes, I knew they were here. Yes, I've seen them. If you must know, I've gone hunting with them – but only to make sure they didn't overdo it. I'm piggy in the middle here – I love my sister but I know what she's like. The Rev is right. We need a plan, but I don't know what we need a plan for, or against. I know she's here, with Olivia in tow, but I don't know why. I have asked but she just laughs and makes jokes that I don't understand."

"What about Julia?" I asked. "Is she responsible for her or was Julia just a genuine natural-causes accident?"

"If she had been found at her home, I would have thought that, but the beach changes everything. That's so Meredith," Aiden replied.

"There's no point wasting time analysing the why," the Rev said. "Let's focus on how we handle this."

Severn stole one of my chips and waggled it in the air. "I'm tempted to go with Riley's suggestion. The show finishes in three days. On Sunday we pack it all up and then, if we need to, we can leave. I am sick of those bitches, so I vote to ignore them. If they do something else dumb and get caught doing it, I don't care." He stood up, picked up his coat and held his hand out to me in an invitation to join him. "Tell you what – you guys can sort out whatever plan you like. You didn't let me in when you first learnt they were here, so if you didn't want me involved before, I'm not getting involved now. Come on, Riley, let's go to your place."

I wanted to hear more but I wasn't going to ruin Severn's dramatic exit, so I grabbed my chips with one hand, took his hand with the other and left.

"Merde!" I heard the Rev swear as we closed the door.

I expected us to walk out to the street but Severn pulled me around the side of the motel and put his fingers to his lips to warn me to be quiet. He pointed to the motel then to his ear and I got the message. He was listening to their conversation now we had left. After a few minutes, he gave a derisive snort and motioned that we should leave, although he reminded me to keep quiet. We sneaked carefully out to the road and walked briskly until we were out of vampire hearing range before Severn spoke.

"Those two are never going to win any awards for precise military-style planning," he said. "Their decision was to go back to the Cerberus tonight and try talking to the girls again. Brilliant!"

"It sounds pretty dumb," I agreed. "You're not going with them? Or after them?"

"Nope. I meant it when I said I don't care." We walked for a while in silence before he spoke again. "Did you really see them at the show tonight?"

"I don't know. It was when I went back to the dressing room to collect the radio mics. I looked up as I was crossing the bridge and thought I saw a shadow behind that big grove of trees, but it might have been just that, a random shadow. I swore at it and got no response, so maybe it wasn't anything."

"Or maybe it was. Now I'm torn. I want to ignore them but, at the same time, I want to know why they are following us. What should I do?"

"Nothing." I stopped, pulling his hand to turn him towards me. "Like you said before, the show finishes in three days then you could be gone again. For ages. Let's just spend the next few days concentrating on us."

"I like that." Severn put his arm around me and pulled me close. I lifted my mouth for his kiss and let the warmth of our emotion chase away any dark thoughts of the girls and their unknown purpose.

We resumed walking, our arms entwined around each other, my head resting against his shoulder. A car racing past us tooted and a voice from inside it yelled, "get a room". Severn laughed and hugged me tighter and I gave them the fingers. We were two normal people on a warm Linwood night.

Walking had always been the best way for me to sort out my thoughts so I let them bounce around in my head as we strolled along. We were nearly home when they started to line themselves up.

"There are at least three separate questions to answer," I said.

"About the girls or about us?"

"The girls. Question one is why are they here. What did they come all this way to do? And I don't believe it was for the nightlife. I doubt Christchurch's Strip is as exciting as Paris, for example."

"True. It's not."

"Question two: did they kill Julia? If they did, is that the answer to question one? Did they come here to do that? And if so, why?"

"Yeah. If they did kill her, it's hardly likely to be random. What's question three?"

"Where do the Rev and Aiden fit in? Are they as confused as we are or are they an integral part of the whole plan? Oh, I guess that makes four questions because there is also why are they keeping you out of the loop?"

"Aarrgghh." Severn let out a long drawn-out moan of despair. "That's the bit that's doing my head in the most. After Seth, while we were away at the monastery and now, back here, it seemed like things had changed. The old balance of Severn at the bottom of the kicking pile had shifted. I really felt we were working as a team. But it seems we are not. We are back to little cliques doing things behind each other's backs and Severn being the last to know anything. You know how you can just be around a group of people too long?"

I nodded. "Yep."

"Well, believe me, a hundred and ten years has been about a hundred and nine years too long for me. I need to do some serious thinking about what happens next."

"Would you leave? Can you leave?"

"Would I? Yes. Can I? That's the million-dollar question. I presume there are solo vampires out there but I don't know how they manage without the support of a group. I may be trapped with these idiots for ever. I wish Finn was here. I could always talk to him. He's a wise old man. He was a wise old man before he was turned and he's seen a lot more since then. I would value his advice right about now."

"Can you contact him? Maybe it would be good if he was here. Aiden and Meredith are his kids, after all. Maybe he could help us sort all this mess out."

Severn stopped walking, spun me towards him and planted a resounding kiss on my forehead.

"You are brilliant! I was thinking I might have to call in Brother Martin but Finn is a much better choice. Or both of them. The Rev won't be happy if I go over his head and call in reinforcements but I have to do something."

"I thought your plan was to ignore them all."

"Yeah, well, I'm not sure I can, even if I want to. But I can ask for help."

He pulled his cell phone from his pocket and pushed a couple of buttons. He must have had the monastery on speed-dial.

"Puis-je parler au Frere Finn, s'il vous plait?" A long pause during which Severn turned to me to explain. "It will be about one o'clock in the afternoon over there so Sext, the midday prayers, will have just finished. Finn will be back down in his workshop, tinkering with something, so it may take them a while to get him to the phone."

"Do you all have to do all the prayers and other monk stuff?"

"No, they let us out of a lot of it, but Finn enjoys it. Says it brings him some balance. I can understand that. Hang on, I can hear footsteps. He's coming." Another pause then he smiled. "Finn, good to hear your voice … yes, unfortunately you are right, I'm not phoning from over here just to chat. We have a bit of a problem …"

Our walking pace slowed as Severn explained the situation to Finn and when we reached home, we perched on our waist-high, stone block fence while they spoke. When the conversation ended he put his phone away and took off his glasses to polish them on the edge of his t-shirt, his expression sombre. He replaced his glasses and pulled his lips back in nasty grin, his fangs partially extended.

"That's put a cat among the pigeons."

"Are you coming in? Staying for a while?" I asked, full of hope but expecting the answer I received.

"No, sorry. I need to go and find a bit of that balance that Finn is always on about. I'm going to find somewhere quiet and sit and think for a few hours. Get some sleep, you need it more than I do. I'll see you tomorrow but it might not be until the afternoon, depending on how and when I feed. Or even if I feed – that's the last thing on my mind at the moment?"

"Whatever you do, stay away from the others."

"I intend to. I don't want to see them or talk to them for a while."

"And if you need to feed, I'm here." I waved my hands to ward off his objections. "I know what the Rev said, I understand it, but if you need blood I'm a safe supply that's not going to add any complications. Plus, if the Rev is right, if you're a bit hungry then we'll get the fun side, not the sleepy side, and I'm all for more of that." I leant forwards to give him a teasingly light kiss. "I'll leave my window unlatched."

CHAPTER TWENTY

Mum woke us in a panic.

Severn had slipped through the window and crawled in beside me about three in the morning. I knew that because I had glanced at my bedside clock as he smoothed my hair out of the way and tantalised me by running a fang lightly over the skin of my neck. We were still curled together when Mum burst through the door.

"Riley! Wake up, you have to see this ... oh, Severn, I'm glad you're here." That wasn't the reaction either of us expected. "You need to see this too. Now! Hurry!" She raced away leaving us gaping at each other, totally bewildered.

Out in the lounge Mum pointed to the television.

"Oh hell, it's the girls." Severn moved to the screen to look closer.

"And Aiden," I added, pointing to the third figure, higher in the sky than the two taking up the majority of the screen.

"Where are they?" Severn squinted at the screen "What building is that?"

"It's the cathedral. In the Square," Mum said. "They're perching just above the entrance like gargoyles. But it gets worse. The cathedral's only one of the places they've been seen. Oh, and in case you hadn't noticed, they're naked."

"Yeah, that is kind of obvious," I said.

"I can appreciate that you can't spread your wings with your clothes on," Mum said, directing herself to Severn, "but surely they could wear a halter top or something? And put on some knickers."

"I doubt either of them has worn knickers for a couple of centuries," Severn replied. "That would cramp their style."

"Well, I hope you don't ... flap everything when you're flapping your wings."

"No way!" Severn laughed at Mum's discomfort. "As you saw, I can flap my wings with my pants on."

"Just as well." Mum pretended to straighten the cushions on the couch to cover the blush I could see creeping up her cheeks.

"Where did the pictures come from?" I asked.

"We're lucky it was dark and whoever took it had a shaky hand

and wavers all over the place," Severn said.

Mum answered my question by turning up the volume. The picture on the screen had cut to a reporter standing in front of the cathedral beside a rotund man whose stomach pushed out over the belt of his taxi driver's uniform. The reporter spoke breathlessly into her oversized microphone.

"Here with me is the man who captured these amazing shots. Salesi Taumalolo was working the late shift and had driven back into the Square when he saw the figures. Salesi, tell us what you saw."

"I don't know." The man twisted his hands nervously and looked everywhere except into the camera. "I don't know what they were. Demons, some kind of demons, flying over the cathedral and laughing, then perching on the top. I just grabbed my phone and started filming. Then I dialled triple 9 and called the cops."

"What happened then?" The reporter prompted him to continue. "What did the police do?"

"Nothing. Those things were gone by the time the police got here. They didn't believe me. I think they thought I was drunk. They were going to breathalyse me until I showed them the pictures on my phone. After that they called the station on their radio and found out there were other calls coming in from all over town." He looked straight into the camera lens. "There's demons loose in Christchurch. Demons. I'm going to church as soon as I leave here. We need to pray. We need the help of Jesus Christ to deliver us from the demons."

"We need the help of some monks from a certain monastery, that's for sure." Severn said. "Just as well they're on their way."

"Who's coming?" Mum asked.

"Finn," Severn replied. "Remember him? The old guy who did floor electrics."

"Oh yes, lovely man."

"Yeah, I figured as he's Aiden and Meredith's father, if anyone can handle them, it's him. I called him last night. And I'm betting Brother Martin, our resident fix-it man, will be with him. For one thing, Martin can fly a plane. Finn can't."

"But your plane is here, at the airport," I pointed out.

"One of our planes is here. We have others."

"Of course you do," Mum said. "Coffee anyone?"

I went with Mum to the kitchen but Severn stayed glued to the television screen. Mum whispered to me while she laid the cups on the bench.

"Will Severn be able to stay now? He won't have to go, will he?"

"No point whispering," I said in a normal voice. "Severn can hear you. Vampires have super-hearing and Severn's is better than most."

"Oh. How far away can he hear us?"

"If I'm on the sound desk, I can hear you backstage," Severn answered from the lounge. "So you need to go at least three houses down the road if you want to talk about me." He joined us in the kitchen with a smile to let Mum know he was teasing her. "I can hear that far but I would have to be specifically listening. Most of the time I let my brain filter it all out, otherwise there would be so much noise in my ears I would go insane. It's part of my hunting skills. I can turn it off."

"You don't miss anything backstage," I said.

"Nope. Because when I'm doing a show I keep my senses alert. I want to be able to pick up any changes in the sound gear and fix them before the audience, or more importantly the stage manager, notices. Riley, turn on your computer – we need to see what social media is making of all this."

I think we all held our collective breath while we waited for my slow computer to lumber into wakefulness. When the social media site loaded, we all stared at it exclaiming variations on "wow", "omg" and a variety of swear words I don't usually hear my mother use.

"Which one is which?" was Mum's first coherent comment. Severn pointed to the screen.

"That's Meredith, above the rose window, and that's Olivia, perched on the peak of the door gable."

"That is Aiden up near the steeple, isn't it?" I asked. "It's not the Rev?"

"No, it's Aiden."

"Look, wait, can you make it go back a couple of seconds," Mum said. Severn complied, clicking the mouse, and as it restarted, Mum pointed to the spectacular silver and blue statue that stood near the cathedral entrance. "There's David, standing down there behind the Chalice, holding Aiden's coat."

"Well, well," Severn rubbed his hands together with a satisfying clap. "Gotcha! All the evidence I needed to show that Aiden and the Rev are right in this up to their necks. Brother Martin is going to love this."

"The religious factions are having a field day," Mum said, scrolling through the comments. "Looks like angels are well and truly off the board and drones are out. It's all demons. Oh, look at this – there's going to be a rally tonight outside the cathedral – prayers and cleansing, it says."

"Crucifixes and pitch forks, more likely," Severn said, his voice a grim growl. "Medieval Europe all over again. That should make the Reverend feel right at home."

I had taken over from Mum scrolling through the comments and stopped to indicate one.

"Look, here's one that argues against the demons. This guy reckons they are BASE jumpers in those flying wing suits."

"Let's hope more people agree with him," Severn said, but he didn't really sound hopeful.

"At least you're not in the picture," Mum said. "That's one good thing."

"That's the only good thing," Severn said. "But, yes, I am so glad I wasn't with them. Mind you, if I had been, I would have got the hell out of there as soon as those girls got airborne."

"Where did you go?" I tried to ask as if it wasn't an interrogation and I wasn't suspicious.

"Edmonds Gardens," Severn said. "I told you I needed to go somewhere quiet and think, so I did. For several hours. It helped. I thought about a lot of stuff and put a few things into perspective. I've got some things to say to the Reverend and some questions for Brother Martin when he arrives, then I have a decision or two to make."

"Are you really going to leave the guild?" I asked.

"I'm not sure. It depends on the answers I get from David and from Brother Martin. I haven't decided yet."

"I just hope this won't affect tonight's show," Mum said. "I hope we still get an audience and people won't be too scared to come out in the dark. Bugger your Brother Martin, if those stupid girls ruin our show, they'll have me to deal with."

Severn grinned at me. "They should go to the rally tonight then, because if your mother goes after them they are going to need all the prayers they can get. God help them."

CHAPTER TWENTY ONE

By mutual agreement, we got to Mona Vale early and were surprised to see Aiden and the Rev waiting for us in the carpark. Neither of them looked happy. Severn thanked Grant for driving us then strode across to the other car, dropping any pretence of polite behaviour as he covered the distance and threw open the driver's door.

"Congratulations! What's your next move? You going to fly into the finale of the show?"

Aiden pushed past him to get out of the car.

"Shut up! I was trying to stop them."

"You failed."

"I know I failed. But at least I tried. Where the hell were you?" Aiden shoved Severn hard in the chest, knocking him back against the car door, and stormed off towards the container.

"Let it go, Severn," the Reverend said as he climbed out of the passenger seat. "Let it go."

I grabbed Severn's arm and tried to steer him away but, as we walked across the carpark, Mum came rushing back.

"This is bad," she said as she ran up to us. "The stage manager is going to have a fit."

"What's happened?" I asked.

"Come and see. All of you. You too David, Aiden. You need to see this."

She rounded us up and herded us down the narrow path towards the flat area that held the stage. We came onto the open grass and stopped in horror. The stage manager was definitely going to have a fit. In the middle of the green where the audience would sit, a group of people stood in a circle, holding hands and singing. But it wasn't the usual pre-show warm-up for the cast. They were chanting something that involved lots of halleluiahs and praise-the-lords while a grey-suited man in their centre held raised hands skywards and shouted for Jesus to protect the cast.

"You know," Severn said, breaking the silence that had descended over us all as we watched the scene, "I have never wanted to be seen flying in public so much. Right now I have this burning urge to take of my t-shirt and fly right into the middle of them."

"Shhh," the Rev grabbed Severn's arm to quieten him and motioned to Mum.

"Don't panic." Severn shook of his hand. "She knows. She's known all the time. We just confirmed it yesterday. Her grandmother knew Seth."

The expression on the Rev's face was priceless.

"Are they cast? Or some kind of weird cult?" I asked.

"Cast, all of them except the bloke in the middle," Mum said.

"What do we do?"

"We start setting up the damned show," a voice behind us answered. I turned to see Danny followed by Cameron pulling the trolley full of lighting gear. "If they get in our road, we go straight through them. We haven't got time for a prayer meeting, we've got a show to rig. Move your backsides, you lot." He paused for a minute then laughed. "Stage manager pulled up a minute ago – she'll move them soon enough."

Which she did. As we stepped aside to let Cameron pull the trolley onto the grass, the stage manager appeared behind us.

"What is this, a crew meditation circle?"

"Yep, meditating what to do about them." Danny pointed to the group in the middle of the lawn.

"You are kidding me," the stage manager said as she took in the scene and realised what was happening. "Who is he and what is he doing with my cast?"

"Praying," I said. "Calling down the heavenly powers to protect us all from the flying demons."

"Well, he can't protect them from me." The stage manager sucked in her breath, squared her shoulders and strode across the grass, her voice rising above the chanting and prayers.

"That's enough!" The cast went quiet instantly. The man in the middle kept praying. As she approached, the circle of cast split like the Red Sea before Moses to let her through until she stood face to face with the pastor. "I said, that's enough!" She turned to the cast. "You lot, backstage now! Warm-ups, costumes, make-up – move it!" The cast scattered and she spun back to the pastor. "You are not part of this show, so you have to leave. Now! Until the audience is allowed in, this place is out of bounds to everyone who is not cast or crew and you are neither. Leave now or I will call security."

Beside me Severn sniggered. We knew there was no security and the ones she would call to remove the pastor would be the crew - exactly the demons he was praying against.

"Go on, make my day, do it, call security," he urged although the stage manager was too far away to hear him. I kind of hoped she would too but in the end the pastor blustered for a few sentences then gave up. To leave he had to pass us – too enticing for the vampires to resist. As he walked through the black-clad guard of honour we formed at the sides of the path, the vampires whispered ominous threats in his ears.

"Watch your back."

"They know where you live."

"Fear the darkness."

The pastor picked up speed and ran, shouting supplications to heaven as he sped towards his car. The stage manager strode back towards us and clapped Severn and Aiden on the back.

"That's it, enough time wasted, pre-show's over. Do as Danny said and get your gear rigged. You've now got forty five minutes and counting."

The lack of time had an advantage – we had no time to argue and no option but to work together to get the set-up completed. Aiden worked like the demon he had been labelled, literally running as he ran out the cables, jogging across the wide lawn with the heavy speakers. By the time the stage manager called "ten minutes to beginners", I was exhausted, even if the vampires still looked fresh as daisies.

In the dressing rooms, as I had handed out the radio mics, I couldn't help but notice the atmosphere. Nobody was chatting about their day. Everyone was quietly applying their make-up or struggling into their costumes in silence, even Mum who was standing in a corner watching the rest of the cast. She whispered to me while I clipped her microphone to her hair.

"Tell the stage manager to come and rev this lot up or the show is going to suck. The energy is all wrong."

I nodded agreement and left the tent to relay her message on my way back to my sound desk where I put on my headphones and started piffling the mics to make sure they were all working. I was jumping from channel to channel, so I heard most of the stage manager's terse telling off followed by her exhortation for the cast to remember the paying audience and raise their game. It was after she left that I heard the conversation that scared me.

I was checking mic ten, one of the extra mics we used on one or two of the strongest singers in the chorus to boost them in the opening and closing numbers, when I caught the words "catch the demons." I reached out to tug Severn's arm then held out my headphones so we could both listen. Severn's expression hardened as the woman spoke.

"The rally will be over by the time we finish here but we're meeting the pastor in the Square," the voice said. "We're going to split into groups and take up positions around the Square, around Latimer Square and down Worcester Boulevard. If they come back tonight, the church will be ready for them."

"How are you going to catch them?" The second woman was keeping her voice purposely quiet but she was close enough to the first woman for us to catch her words through the mic.

"We don't have to catch them," the voice said. "We just need to lure them close enough. One of our church members is a professional cricketer. He's got a good bowling arm and he says that if he can get close enough he can hit them with these special balls he's been making today. Tennis balls wrapped in rags, soaked in petrol. Burning petrol. We'll send them back to the hell they came from."

Severn reached over to push the PFL button, cutting off the feed. He sat back in his chair, wide-eyed with shock.

"No. No matter what I think of the girls, that is one nasty way to go. " He raised his voice slightly. "Rev, Aiden, I know we're almost on standby but we've just heard some threats against the girls. Come here as soon as we get past the opening number."

CHAPTER TWENTY TWO

The Rev demanded to know exactly which cast member it was so he could inflict some damage and Aiden wanted to find the pastor and "clean him up". We compromised. I pointed out the chorus member wearing microphone number ten and the Rev promised to follow her after the show, without inflicting bodily harm. The Rev said he could easily help us pack the gear while she changed out of her costume and removed her make-up, and we agreed he would leave to follow her when she left. Not that it would matter too much if he lost her, we knew they were heading to the Square so he could still find her – especially as they would be waiting a long time for their demons.

Aiden made sure he could also identify the singer as his superior sense of smell could help to pinpoint her among the rest of her group. His first priority, though, would be to locate the girls and warn them but we all knew the girls well, so we fully expected their reaction would be to fly into the Square on purpose.

During interval Aiden and I went to the women's dressing room. I needed to talk to Mum and Aiden had thought of a way to get close to Mic Ten Wearer so he could identify her individual smell.

"I need to check your mic pack," he said to her. "If you can just turn around, I need to check the batteries."

"No, absolutely not," the singer replied, slapping Aiden's outstretched hand away.

"Sound desk has reported that it's cutting out," Aiden said, keeping his voice calm. "I need to check it."

"No. You are not touching me. I am not having a strange man touch my body Go away! Her" She pointed to me. "She can check it. You can stand over there."

"I'm busy," I called back. "You can trust Aiden, he's a professional, not some pervert creep." Well, not when he's working, anyway.

She started to object again but Mum stepped forwards in her exasperated mother mode and addressed the girl. "Oh, for heaven's sake! Sorry, dear, but you need to get over yourself. You have a lovely voice but this is musical theatre. You need to be less of a prude if you ever want to move out of the chorus line. I can vouch for Aiden and all the other men on the crew. You need to think of them like you would your doctor. He's interested in the battery in the microphone pack, not in your tush."

With that, she spun the girl around, hoisted up her skirt and fished out the pack from where it was pinned to her underwear. Aiden, keeping his expression serious and his eyes down, made a play of replacing the perfectly fine batteries and handed it back to Mum who replaced it with far less finesse than Aiden would have used, pulled the girl's skirt back into position and returned to her own end of the dressing room. Mic Ten Wearer looked furious, embarrassed and humiliated all at once. Mum was trying not to laugh.

Keeping my voice low, I told Mum what I had heard. When she realised that Aiden's battery change had been for some other purpose, after glaring at Mic Ten Wearer, she pulled me outside the tent to ask what the vampires were going to do. I reminded her about Aiden's heightened sense of smell and how he had used it to uncover Tommy's kidnapper and explained their plan to follow her into the Square. Mum decided on a more direct approach, took her phone, found a quiet spot away from the dressing room where she wouldn't be disturbed, and called the police.

"They said they were already planning to have a presence watching the rally and weren't too interested until I mentioned the flaming petrol-soaked balls. That got their attention. Our famous cricketer might find himself in the headlines tomorrow if he tries to bowl any," Mum reported as we returned to the dressing room.

I said goodbye and dashed back to the sound desk to tell Severn and the others what Mum had done. Severn and the Rev agreed she had done the right thing and were grateful but Aiden sulked as if she had spoilt his fun. She probably had.

The show was the worst one for the season with a meagre audience and a dispirited cast and we all heaved a sigh of relief when it was over. The equipment was packed up in record time; the vampires anxious to find the girls and the lighting guys keen to check out the rally.

"If we're lucky, the demons will turn up," Cameron said. "I want to get a good look. Did you notice they were stark naked?"

A free peep show – good on ya, Cameron.

The Rev took off on foot, following a group of actors, including

Mic Ten Wearer, who were walking into the city through Hagley Park. Aiden stayed with us so Severn could drive him close to the Cerberus nightclub. Mum wisely decided her best move was to stop Grant going into the Square, no matter how badly he wanted to see the flying demons for himself. She tried to convince him that it was all hype and finally told him about the potential violence of the pastor's group to get him to see sense and go home. While he was loading their stage bags into their car, Mum came over to where Severn and I were standing with Aiden.

"Are you two going to be all right? Will you promise me you will stay safe?"

"I promise," I said.

"I'll keep us both safe," Severn said. "Riley's lucky she can't fly and if I have to go in to help the others, I'll fly high."

"Yes, and keep your face out of camera range. Oh, hang on, I've got an idea. Wait a minute." She ran back to their car and rummaged in the book, returning to us with a balaclava-style beanie which she held out to Aiden. "Here. If you have to fly, pull this over your face. Sorry, Severn, I've only got one but if you both need to fly at once, wrap this around your face." She handed Severn Grant's red and black rugby scarf.

"Thanks. With my own beanie pulled down and this, I should be able to stay incognito. Awesome idea."

"Yeah, thanks Mrs W," Aiden said, pulling the balaclava over his head. "Just call me Batman."

With a groan at his sad attempt at humour, Mum exhorted us again to be careful and they drove away, leaving the three of us alone in the carpark. At our car, Aiden dumped his coat on the back seat, suggesting that Severn do the same.

"We can't fly in them and we can't drop them in the gutter or we'll never see them again."

"What about your t-shirts. Will you need me to hold those if you fly?" I asked.

"Nah, I'll tuck mine in my belt. That way, I can pull it on quickly if I have to land and blend in."

"That makes sense."

We drove down Riccarton Avenue, swung into Montreal Street and deposited Aiden on the corner of Oxford Terrace, then continued down Hereford Street to find a park closer to the Square. Severn and I approached the Square through a small alley which took us by the back of the cathedral, and made our way around the edge until we could see the Square's central courtyard and the huge crowd gathered there, praying and chanting.

"Let's add a prayer," Severn said. "Let's pray Aiden finds the girls and keeps them well away from here tonight."

"Amen to that," I agreed. "And let's pray that the winged angels from the mountain get here speedily in their heavenly chariot, or whatever you call your 'other' jet." I stressed 'other' to get in a dig as I still found it hard to comprehend anyone who had not one but several planes at their disposal.

Severn looked at his watch. "I called Finn about eleven o'clock last night. Assuming it took them a couple of hours to get packed, get to the airport and get flight clearance, and allowing for a couple of refuelling stops on the way, it's about a twenty-one hour flight, so I reckon they will be here by one or two in the morning. Or before, depending on how direct a route Martin choses to take."

"Only two hours to get from the monastery to Paris? I thought you were way down in the south somewhere."

"We are. We fly out of Toulouse-Blagnac airport. There is more than one international airport in France, you know."

"Oops. I'm hopeless at geography."

Severn put his arm around me and pulled me close. "At least you can navigate us around the Square. We really need to get over to the other side without getting into the middle of the mob or stopped by the police."

"Follow me."

We skirted around the perimeter of the Square, hugging the walls of the shops that framed it, trying to stay in the darkest patches. We got to the Worcester Boulevard intersection before Severn spotted the group of cast members, including the Rev watching from a safe distance behind them. Severn said something I didn't pick up but I saw the Rev look our way and raise his hand in recognition. We didn't attempt to join him, but took up a position where we could follow any part of the group that split off in our direction.

"Can you see the cricketer guy?" Severn asked.

"I wouldn't know a cricketer from a hole in the ground," I said. "We would need Grant for that. But my guess would be the tall, skinny guy carrying the large sports bag that's probably full of dangerously soggy tennis balls."

The police must have thought the same thing. Or they knew

what he looked like.

The rally had been going for at least an hour before we got there and was starting to lose its momentum. The preachers taking centre stage on their temporary raised dais on the cathedral steps were tag-teaming each other, rotating their turn as whoever was yelling started to lose their voice, but their message was all the same. Lots of biblical out-of-context quotes, dire warnings about satanic minions, and prayers that were answered by the crowd in a torrent of halleluiahs. After the first five minutes I was bored, which is why I noticed the police closing in. We weren't the only ones sneaking into the event incognito. I gave Severn a nudge.

"That guy moving in, the one just in front of the two cops in uniform, he's the cop who interviewed me for hours about Tasha."

We shrank back into the protective shadow of the building and watched the police contingent approach the group containing the cast members. Behind them, I saw the Rev walk away. He had heard my comment and taken evasive action. The uniformed police halted and the plain-clothes detective stepped forwards to tap the tall skinny guy on the shoulder. The cricketer turned around with a welcoming smile for whoever had approached him. The smile sank to a quizzical frown as the detective said words I couldn't hear and held out his warrant card, then the cricketer's expression changed a third time, the frown twisting to fury. The detective indicated the sports bag and the cricketer bolted.

Clutching the bag to his chest, he spun on his heel and attempted to break through the crowd of supporters behind him. The uniformed police sprang after him but the crowd was on his side, blocking and hampering the police pursuit. Our corner of the rally soon became a riot, the police shoving people aside as they rushed to overwhelm the fleeing cricketer while the members of our cast and their friends fought back. With angry shouts, they snatched at the police, pulling at their vests and trying to surround them or trip them up. In the middle of the melee I spotted Mic Ten clinging to the back of a policewoman, pulling at her hair and screaming. I pointed her out to Severn who gave a derisive snort.

"Pity she doesn't project her voice that well on stage. She wouldn't need a microphone," he said. "And it looks like she won't need one tomorrow. She's just been arrested."

Behind the policewoman handcuffing Mic Ten, the cricketer was still on the move, dodging backwards and forwards, sidestepping the police and taking advantage of the gaps in the crowd created by his supporters. But as he ran further towards the centre of the rally, he outran his friends and found himself trapped in the dense, swaying mass of people in prayer. A woman rocking a pram forced the cricketer to change direction, and he ran straight into the arms of another police officer coming in on a flanking manoeuvre. Some of the rally stopped praying to applaud as the policeman dragged him away.

Duly handcuffed, the cricketer was marched back to the detective who reached out to accept the bag that the cricketer had determinedly held onto. As the detective reached forwards to open the bag to display the weapons inside, the rally broke into to a rousing chorus of perfectly-timed halleluiahs. I never thought I would credit that annoying detective with good work but that was well executed. Pity Mum wasn't there to see it.

CHAPTER TWENTY THREE

More police, including several with dogs straining on their leashes and barking at the now terrified crowd, spread out through the Square. As they made their presence obvious, the rally fell apart. None of the well-meaning, scared folk who had genuinely feared the arrival of the demons wanted to be arrested for praying, so they dispersed faster than crew when the stage manager called for a volunteer. One minute we were standing at the back of the rally, well out of the road, and the next we were engulfed in a tsunami of people, running, crying, still praying. A thousand or more people all swarmed at once into the narrow opening of Worcester Boulevard, where we were standing.

We pressed ourselves back against the wall of the shop behind us but there was nowhere to go. The crowd was relentless, surging into the street opening, and spreading out towards us as they ran out of space. Someone was pushed against me and I lost contact with Severn. The tide of humanity surged again and I was swept into it, away from him. I heard him call my name but I couldn't fight against the determined flow. A woman shoved me hard against the building as she forced her way past me. I stumbled, clutching at her to regain my balance but, instead of helping me, she swung her fist. My head rocked backwards into the building's window frame, my vision blurred and I sank to the ground.

Nothing made sense. Lights seemed to flash all around me, my head was exploding with pain and when I raised my hand to feel my head, my hand came away wet which I couldn't understand. My head was spinning and I wasn't sure where I was or why I was so cold. I tried to stand up but a strong hand on my shoulder held me down.

"Don't try to move, love," a gentle voice said. "You've had a nasty bash on your head and you're bleeding. Just take it easy."

I sat back against the cold stone of the building and let my brain re-engage. Gradually the flashing lights behind my eyes faded and I could see that the liquid on my hands was, as the voice had said, my own blood. I looked up. The crowd had moved on but crouched beside me were two men. Severn knelt to my left, his arm around my shoulder, and to my right the owner of the gentle voice, a police officer looking anything but gentle in a protective riot vest.

"You got punched in the face and then hit your head on the stonework," Severn explained. "You've got a cut on your head and you're going to have a black eye by tomorrow. How do you feel?"

"Do you need me to call an ambulance?" the policeman asked.

"I'll be fine," I assured him. "It hurts but it's not worth an ambulance."

"It's still a head injury. You need to be checked out," the policeman insisted. "I don't want you walking away then collapsing later."

"I could take her to the hospital," Severn said. "Our car is just over in Hereford Street. If you could sit with her, I could run and get it."

"All right," the policeman agreed. "As long as you make sure you go to the hospital, or at least to the after hours surgery."

"I will. Riley, I'll be right back. Don't move."

"Riley, is it?" the policeman asked as Severn jogged away. "Is that young lad your boyfriend?"

"Yes," I said with pride.

"And what were you two doing down here tonight? Were you part of the rally?"

"No, we were just passing through the Square. I guess we were being a bit nosy so we stopped to watch for a while."

"So you weren't with any of the groups there tonight?"

"No."

"Your boyfriend? He wasn't here to meet the National Front?"

"What? The National Front. Aren't they the white power lot? Why would you think we were meeting them?"

"Your black clothes, his haircut. Looks pretty National Front to me."

"No, no no. We're theatre crew. We're with the Robin Hood show that's running in Mona Vale at the moment. We had a performance tonight and we came here after the show finished. We wear black so the audience don't notice us and we haven't had time to get changed yet. We do the sound, the microphones and all that. I can get our stage manager to vouch for us, if we need it."

"Theatre crew, eh? So if I came to the show tomorrow, just to check, where would I find you two?"

"On the shorter of the two scaffolding towers, behind the sound desks. Or running around the dressing rooms attaching radio microphones to actors. You can always check with Grant Watson who plays the Sherriff – he's my stepfather."

"Okay, I believe you. Now, where's your boyfriend with that car?"

We sat in silence for a few more minutes before Severn pulled up, then the policeman helped me to my feet and into the passenger seat. I thanked him for looking after me and we drove off.

"He thought we were National Front members because of our blacks and your ultra-short haircut," I said.

"You should have said no, all vampires look like this. Now, how do we get to the hospital?"

"Do we have to?"

"Yes we do. He's right. You had two blows to your head. I'm not going to be the one who has to explain to your mother if you've got a concussion and I don't get you checked out."

At the hospital the Accident and Emergency Department was full of rally-goers with a range of injuries from sprains and cuts to broken bones and one serious knife wound. He and the group with him were definitely National Front as their jacket patches proclaimed so we weren't surprised when our black clothes got us dirty looks as we entered. We could have done without being shadowed by a massive security guard who watched us with suspicion as we waited to be seen.

At Severn's suggestion, I rang Mum while Sev sent texts to Aiden and the Rev. Mum wanted to rush straight into the hospital but I managed to convince her that I wasn't too badly hurt. I blamed Severn and the policeman for being over-cautious and I downplayed the truth – that my head ached and my eye had swollen up. We were still waiting to see a doctor when the Rev and Aiden arrived, their black clothes getting them the evil eye from the security guard.

"Where are the girls?" Severn demanded as they slumped into seats beside us.

"Safe from that angry lot tonight," Aiden replied. "They're still in the club. Olivia was all for flying over the rally and dropping buckets of glitter over them but, for once in her life, Meredith got sensible. Apparently, and I am only quoting her and have no idea what she means, they have bigger fish to fry and need to save their energy. When I left them a few minutes ago they were eyeing up some poor sucker to be their dinner so we can safely assume they won't be leaving the club for another hour or so."

"Good," I said. "I hope they don't. I could be stuck here for another hour or so too. My head hurts so you guys can do the thinking for a change. Aiden, you must have some idea what those girls are up to. You're Meredith's twin. She must have said something that would give us a hint. Think, man."

"Let's backtrack," Severn suggested. "Last we knew, the girls were in the monastery and didn't seem to have any great desire to come back here. What changed that?"

"We came," Aiden said. "Riley sent us some emails and we decided to fly out and help."

"And we discussed it. We talked about it in front of the girls when you were packing your suitcase," the Rev added. "Remember Aiden? The girls were there too."

"Yeah, they were. What did they ask us again?"

After a pause the Rev answered. "Meredith asked if it was Riley's company – well, actually she called Riley Severn's bitch but we won't go there. I said yes because I hadn't clicked that it was a different company with Riley's lot helping out. I wasn't really listening to them, because they talk rubbish all the time and my mind was working on another level, trying to work out the logistics of our journey, and I walked away. They were still speaking but I wasn't listening, sorry."

"Hang on, I'm trying to remember," Aiden said. "Give me a minute." He steepled his fingers and bounced them off each other for what seemed like forever before he spoke again. "Olivia asked if they could come too. I said no. Meredith asked why not and whined a bit, trying to use the little girly begging voice that worked on Finn when she was a kid. I told her no again and she called me something rude. I zipped up my bag and pushed them out of my room and they went the other way to me but I heard Olivia whisper about going anyway. She said something else, what was it?" He paused to think, dragging the memory from the back of his brain. "You need to find her. She still owes you. That's what she said."

"Who's the she?" the Rev asked. "Riley?"

"I don't think so. She doesn't like Riley, mainly because Riley's with Severn and she doesn't like Severn winning anything, but she doesn't hate her. She's sort of ambivalently negative."

"Much the same as I feel about her," I said.

"So who is she after?" the Rev repeated.

"Julia," I said. "It had to be Julia. It all fits. Julia is dumped on the beach with nothing to show how she got there, which suggests to me that she was flown there. At her funeral we found out that during our last show, the first time you guys were here, she was one of Seth's hook-ups and was pretty cut up when he left without saying goodbye."

"Which was our fault," Severn said. "I wish we'd known. I would have faked a letter from him."

"Anyway," I continued. "We might not have known but I reckon Meredith and Olivia did. Those two were Seth's acolytes. He didn't go anywhere without them. I think they were jealous of Julia."

"But Seth flirted with everybody. Why would Julia make them more jealous than any other one of the hundreds of women he's flirted with?"

"Because he wanted to turn her," Aiden said. "He wanted to add her to his collection. Neither of them would have wanted that."

"What makes you think that?" the Rev asked.

"Because Seth mentioned it. We were out hunting. Severn, you and the girls had gone into a club to pick up a punter and you, Rev, had got distracted by something, can't remember what, so there was just Seth and me standing in some alleyway. He asked me what I would think of turning another girl. I knew Riley was always chatting with you two, so I thought he was talking about her. He said no, he meant a girl on his side of the stage. That had to be Julia."

"She was certainly in love with him," I said. "She was deeply depressed when he didn't say goodbye. See, it all fits together. The girls are still holding a grudge against Julia for stealing their man and came back for revenge. I still don't get the Brighton beach fetish though."

"None of us understand that," Aiden said. "None of us has ever understood that."

"If that's true, they've achieved their mission, so why are they still here causing all this trouble? Why haven't they just gone back to France?" the Rev asked.

"Because they're bored silly in France," Aiden said. "It's a monastery, for heaven's sake. It might be perfect for the old monks and not too bad for a computer geek like Severn, but those two are party animals. They're not going to go back there voluntarily. They didn't go there voluntarily to start with. You'll need chains and shackles to get them back there again."

The Rev fiddled with his ponytail while he considered his options.

"Well, they can't stay here. They've caused too much trouble for that. I wonder if we can cut a deal with them. I'm sure we can fund them to move somewhere else, like Paris, or New York."

"That could work. They might go for that, let's try it. We got through the whole anti-demon rally without them flying in just to stir things up, so maybe I can reason with them. If that's a serious offer, Rev, let me take it to them."

"No, we'll both go. It needs to come directly from me," the Rev said.

"In that case, you don't need us," Severn said. "I'll stay here with Riley, then get her home. Keep me posted via text, okay?"

"Okay," they said in unison.

"Good luck with the girls and try to keep them grounded."

The Rev and Aiden left us, their exit shadowed by the guard who followed them out the door.

"Did we jump the gun calling Finn?" I asked when they were out of hearing range. "Have we dragged them all this way for nothing?"

"Maybe. I will feel pretty bad if we have. The Rev is going to be really angry with me because he's the boss and I have completely distrusted him and undermined his authority. I think Seven has just dropped himself back to the bottom of the kicking pile."

"When I get out of here, should we drive out to the airport and meet Finn and Martin?"

"Hmm. I should take you home but yeah, why not. If we are stuck here much longer, they will have touched down. But only if you're up to it and the doctor says it's okay. You wouldn't rather go home and get some sleep?"

"Compromise. You drive to the airport, I'll sleep in the car. You can wake me when they arrive."

CHAPTER TWENTY FOUR

The doctor had other ideas. When I was finally seen, I was run through a series of tests, asked lots of questions and sent for an x-ray. After another long wait, I was wheeled into a different room and told I had to stay there for several hours until they were sure I wasn't concussed. Severn wanted to stay but I told him to call Mum then sent him away. Meeting Finn and Brother Martin was more important. A nurse had given me painkillers and all I wanted to do was sleep, so Severn agreed to collect me in a few hours, if Mum didn't get there first.

When they finally released me and I walked out the hospital door, the dawn was breaking. I had spent the last few hours trying to sleep but being woken at regular intervals by nurses asking me what was my name, who was the Prime Minister — dumb but necessary questions to make sure my brain was functioning. Mum must have arrived at some stage as she was sitting beside me, but I must have been asleep as I didn't see her arrive.

Eventually the doctor reappeared, declared me not concussed and signed my release papers, freeing Mum and I to go home and find some decent coffee.

"Where did Severn go?" Mum asked as we drove eastwards. "I expected him to be glued to your bedside."

"He needed to go to the airport," I said. "Finn and Brother Martin should be here by now."

"I imagine they have a lot to discuss, so let's leave them to it and just worry about you. What happened?"

I spent the rest of the drive home filling Mum in on the evening, starting with the dramatic arrest of the cricketer. My description of Mic Ten's attack on the policewoman got a typical Mum reaction — she was more concerned about who would sing the woman's high soprano notes in tonight's show than about the fate or condition of Mic Ten.

"But how did you get injured? Were you in the middle of it all?" she asked.

I explained about the rally becoming a panic and how I had been crushed against the wall as the crowd surged forwards, then hit in the face by a crazy woman. When I told her the policeman had thought we were National Front, she laughed but I could see she was horrified at the same time and that amused me. Her daughter dabbling in extreme politics was a shocking thought, but hanging out with vampires was okay.

As soon as we arrived home I headed for the shower to wash away the blood that was sticking to my hair in matted clumps. I looked at myself in the mirror and immediately understood why the policeman had been so insistent I go to the hospital. I looked like a zombie. My blood-soaked hair was sticking out in bloodied dreads around the large bandage a nurse had applied, and more blood had trickled in rivers down my neck and over my face onto my clothes. My left eye was swollen shut, the surrounds dark and purple. A tentative feel of my head where the bandage was told me it hurt. How was I going to wash off the blood without opening the wound again? I called Mum for help.

Mum found a stool and sat me in the shower, gently washing my hair with warm water, then applied a new dressing and bandage and bundled me into my pyjamas. I was snuggled on the couch in a rug, listening to Mum scrubbing the blood off my blacks, when Severn arrived, by himself.

"Did you meet Finn and Martin?" I asked after I had assured him I didn't feel as bad as I looked.

"Yes. We had a long talk. About a lot of stuff."

"Where are they? Have they gone to the motel?"

"No. We found a quiet corner at the airport and talked there. I showed them the video of the girls and Aiden flying over the cathedral and they were not impressed. I told them everything that happened last night at the rally and I stressed that Aiden had done a good job keeping the girls from doing anything stupid. Aiden might be an idiot, and he doesn't always think things through, but under all that bravado there's a good guy. I mean, anyone who would willingly turn into a vampire to help his sister must have a good heart."

"Did you tell them about the offer the Rev was going to make to the girls?"

"Yes, and I apologised if I had overstepped the Rev's authority and brought them here needlessly if the Rev had it under control. Brother Martin made a rather derogatory comment about the Rev's ability to control anything and told me some news he is planning on delivering to the Rev later today. David might own the monastery, but he's about to be demoted as Grand Master. They think they were hasty in offering him the position and Brother Martin is carrying a warrant officially relinquishing him of the title."

"Why did they make him Grand Master in the first place?" Mum had overheard the last part of our conversation. "Was it just because he owns the land?"

"I asked the same question," Severn replied. "It's because he's a father, not just a brother."

"What's the difference?" I asked.

"The monks who joined the order to be monks are brothers but if they are actually ordained as a priest, they are a father, and apparently that's the way the Guild has always run. The Grand Master has always been an ordained priest. David was the only one who hadn't had a turn at being Grand Master, so they gave him the job because none of the others wanted it back."

"Is he really an ordained priest?" Mum asked. "Seriously? I thought that Rev thing was just a joke."

"Nope. No joke. He is really the Reverend Father David Rochester. Well, actually, the Reverend Father Daveed – to pronounce it correctly – Rocheforte, the Rochester is his anglicised version for outside the monastery."

"When are they going to tell him?" I asked.

"Tonight. They're vampires. Unlike me, they've never got the hang of daylight. They're going to hole up somewhere and sleep all day. Finn said they are going to come to the show tonight and watch, because Finn loves theatre and is missing being backstage, but without being seen as they don't want Aiden or the Rev to know they're here until afterwards. I have to get us all together after everyone else has left, then they will get all formal and Brother Martin will take over and start giving orders."

"How are they going to deal with the girls? They're not going to be at the show."

"They were the other night, creeping around in the bushes. Fortunately, dealing with them is not going to be my problem. I am more than happy to let Brother Martin and Finn handle them. I'm more worried about you. And I'm being completely selfish when I say that. If you're not okay, I'm going to have to handle both desks by myself, so you'd better be up and raring to go by show time. I don't want to have to deal with the musicians. I hate musicians."

"Don't say that around Anita and Caleb," I said. "He's just been accepted into the Youth Orchestra with his violin. And Anita plays the flute."

"Okay, I'll modify that. I only hate musicians who bump my microphones and who want their volume turned up. I don't hate all musicians. Flutes are okay. I like flutes. And bagpipes. I love bagpipes. I've been tempted to get a set and play them from the monastery roof. A haunting piobaireachd or two would stir up the locals on a full moon."

"What's a peebrock ? Can you really play the bagpipes?"

"A sad tune and yes, believe it or not, I can. I'm from Scotland, remember?"

"Pity you can't fly and play the bagpipes at the same time," Mum said. "Imagine what the demon hunters would make of that."

Severn laughed. "It's hard enough to co-ordinate breathing, pumping and fingering all at the same time without adding wing flapping and staying airborne. I think I'll pass on trying that."

Mum got serious. "Severn, if Riley is going to make it to the show tonight, she needs some rest. Much as we love your company, you need to disappear and let her have a few hours' sleep. Off to bed, young lady."

Severn kissed me goodbye and I did as Mum ordered, drifting off to sleep almost immediately. When I woke up again, it was mid-afternoon. My head still ached but I felt strong and energetic, ready and willing to handle my share of the show's workload. I dressed in the freshly laundered blacks that Mum had laid on the end of my bed, brushed my hair carefully around the glaring white bandage and stared at my garish reflection in the mirror. At least I didn't have to go on stage.

In the kitchen, Mum handed me a coffee and pointed to the newspaper on the table. The famous cricketer was now infamous, his arrest in handcuffs making banner headlines. The accompanying photograph was a slightly burred shot from someone's phone but a note under it directed us to page three which held a montage of other photos showing the preaching, the praying and the panic in glorious technicolour. There were no vampires in any of the pictures.

CHAPTER TWENTY FIVE

My pack-in at the show was a lot slower than normal as I had to pause every few minutes to repeat the explanation for my black eye. At least the bandage was hidden under my beanie. I kept my answers simple, only giving a full explanation to the stage manager who wanted to be sure I was well enough to be on the crew. When I told her what had happened she slapped me lightly on the back.

"Good on you, I like your attitude. The show must go an and all that. You'll be right. Worse things happen at crew parties."

Mic Ten Wearer had made it to the show too. When I had survived the men's barrage of questions about my black eye, I found the women's dressing room about to erupt into an argument. Mic Ten was holding court about her treatment in the cells overnight and how despicable the police were to arrest her when she was attending a peaceful prayer meeting, while her friends were still raving about the demons and saying how brave she had been to stand up for the rights of her church group. Mum, Heidi McCormack and some of the other ladies were desperately trying to carry on with their usual backstage routines and ignore them, but I could feel the rising tension as I entered with their microphones.

I have a lower garbage tolerance than my mother. I had tucked microphone ten into the ranting woman's belt pack and was running the wire up her back when yet another comment about the evil demons, combined with the raspy tone of her voice that did not help my nagging headache, flicked my anger switch.

"At least the demons didn't punch anyone in the face, attack any police or carry a bag full of petrol bombs. That was all you lot. Peace, love, prayer and petrol bombs. Praise the Lord!"

A round of applause started by Heidi followed me as I turned and walked away, holding my head as high as I could. In the stunned silence, I heard Mum and Heidi take over, ordering the trouble-makers to be quiet and cajoling the others to ignore them.

"How are they back there?" the stage manager asked as I passed her station.

"Still in demon mode," I said. "But I either just shut it down or made it worse. Hope it wasn't the latter."

With a smile that was anything but benign, the stage manager put down her headphones and stood up.

"I'd better go and give them my nightly get-your-act-together talk, then. Fifteen minutes to beginners."

I got back to my tower and climbed to my desk to find it covered in a bunch of flowers and three bars of chocolate. The flowers were obviously stolen from the nearby gardens and had been tied together by gaffer tape. The note taped to it had a large hand-drawn heart and was signed by Danny and Cameron. I could see them watching me from the top of their tower so I waved and blew them a kiss.

"The chocolate is from Aiden," Severn told me when he arrived a few minutes later. "He feels bad that you got hurt because of something his sister started."

"Thanks, Aiden," I said, knowing he would hear me.

I picked up my pen and wrote 'any sign of Finn?' on the corner of my script. Severn shook his head. I shrugged – an unspoken gesture to show I was willing to accept that I didn't know what was going on - and we settled in to wait for the call to start the show. My headphones did not help my headache. They were the kind we preferred, with only one ear covered by a padded cushion, but I couldn't swap the cushion to my other ear, on the side of my head that hadn't connected with a wall, as that put the attached microphone at the wrong angle, and having the unpadded piece of band that held the headphones on digging into the injured side of my head was just as painful. I fiddled with the placing of the cushion and finally slid my left hand underneath it to hold it away from my ear, hoping I could work the board with just my right hand.

By the end of the show, I was exhausted, aching, and a bit nauseous. Mum wanted to scoop me up and take me home to bed, but she knew what was going to happen and understood that I wanted to be there, no matter how bad I was feeling. With a warning to be careful, she left me packing up the equipment and went home with Grant. I thanked Danny and Cameron again for the flowers, kissed them both on the cheek, which made Cameron blush, and waved as they drove away. Now it was just us, just me and a pack of vampires, alone in the dark.

"Did you manage to put your offer to Meredith and Olivia?"

Severn asked the Reverend.

"Yes, I did. We caught up with them. They were still at the nightclub. I made my offer and they countered by asking for two houses, one in Paris and one in New York, and a larger allowance than I had anticipated. I agreed to both and they agreed to consider it. In fact, they said they would meet us here tonight to let me know their decision."

"I didn't trust them," Aiden said. "They agreed too easily. While you were speaking, Rev, I was watching the looks they were giving each other. I don't know. My twin vibe was picking up something from Meredith. I just don't know what."

"As long as they agree to pack up and get out of here, I don't care what else is on their agenda," the Rev said.

"Two houses and an allowance, which will go on forever?" Severn asked. "Can the Guild afford that? Don't you have to get that approved?

"I'm not asking the Guild to afford it," the Rev replied. "I'm funding this myself, out of my own pocket. I already own property in both cities and I can afford their lifestyle as I don't spend much on my own. I figure it's the least I could do. If I had done better with Seth, none of this would have happened."

"That's dead right." Finn's voice came from behind the trees.

Aiden rushed forwards to hug his father as the two newcomers emerged but the Rev stood his ground, folding his arms tightly against his chest, his body language defensive.

"Brother Martin," he said, his clipped speech reflecting his suspicion. "What brings you here. Or rather, who brought you here?" He glared at Severn who remained impassively poker-faced.

"I brought us here, at Finn's request," Brother Martin replied, his delicate French accent softening the authority behind his voice. "He watches the news while you are here. He knows the girls have come here also. He sees the pictures. He asks my advice. So we come. This is not a good thing that is happening. We cannot allow it."

I was relieved to hear them cover for Severn. No mention at all of our desperate phone call. The Reverend blustered.

"It's under control. It was unfortunate but I've got it sorted. We've only got two more days here anyway. Riley's show finishes tomorrow night. You've had a wasted trip."

"No, I do not think so," Brother Martin said. "It is not under control and nothing has been under control for quite some time. We have much to discuss. The council has already been in discussion as they are full of concern. It is good that you have made an offer to control the two girls and we hope that they will accept it, but whether they do or they do not, there is more we need to address."

Severn put his arm around me and drew me back a couple of paces away from the group. I could feel his muscles twitching as his protective hunting mode kicked in. I looked across at Finn and Aiden, standing side by side. Finn had his arm around Aiden's shoulder offering fatherly support but his straight back suggested he, too, was on the alert as Brother Martin pulled a folded piece of paper from his pocket and handed it to the Rev. I held my breath.

The Rev read the document, held it up to show us and burst into a raucous cackle of laughter.

"I've been demoted," he said, a wide grin stretching across his face. "Brother Martin, that is the best news I have had for a long time."

"You are not disappointed? You are not angry?" Brother Martin asked, incredulous.

"No, not at all, quite the contrary," the Rev replied. "I hate the job. I am hopeless at it. There are at least six other men far better suited to it than I am. This is such a huge relief. I was wondering how I could give it up. I was going to call an emergency meeting next week, when I'm back at the monastery, and beg you guys to let me quit. Oh, thank you, thank you, a thousand times thank you."

"What will you do now?" Brother Martin asked, thrown off his planned speech by the Rev's unexpected response.

"What I'm good at. What all of us here are good at. Severn, Aiden, myself, and Riley of course, make one hell of a good theatre crew. I just want to keep doing that."

"What about the offer to the girls? Will that still stand if you're not Grand Master?" Aiden asked.

"Absolutely. Like I said before, it's coming out of my pocket. I can still afford it. All we need now is for the girls to accept it."

CHAPTER TWENTY SIX

"I am glad you are so confident," Brother Martin said. "I, maybe, am not so much but we will wait. And while we do, I will say that I am impressed by the precision in which you all work at your theatre tasks. You have good work ethics, all of you. I can now understand why you are so much requested."

"I loved the show," Finn said. "Good timing on your sound effects, Severn. Nicely done."

"The Friar does not quite wear his habit correctly," Brother Martin said, which made us all laugh, "but the fighting with the staves was excellent. They have been taught well."

"My best friend's boyfriend's father taught them," I said, watching the confusion on Brother Martin's face as he figured out the relationship.

Beside me, Severn relaxed out of his hunting mode, grinning at Brother Martin's language barrier. Finn, too, had pulled back as he talked about the show.

"So tell me how they did the arrow trick?" he asked. "How did Robin Hood hit that target so precisely?"

"Was he not just a good shot?" Brother Martin asked.

"No, it had to be a stage trick," Finn said. "Back in the day, when I was young and fit, I could have made that shot multiple times, but I know all the health and safety regulations these guys have to go through, so I'm betting it was an illusion."

"You bet right," I said. "It's on a wire. Come up to the stage and I'll show you. It's a neat trick, you'll love it."

With everyone following like sheep, I led the way down the narrow path and across the open lawn to the stage. In the dark the cardboard and corflute castle looked foreboding, its fake turrets looking real as they loomed ominously over us.

"Up here," I said to Finn as I climbed the steps at the side of the stage. He followed me but the others stayed on the grass, not interested in the theatre prop. Finn, however, was fascinated. I showed him the hook that held the invisible wire in place until it was released and the tiny pulley system that pulled the arrow at lightning speed across the stage and through the centre of the brightly coloured target.

"I figured it had to be something like that," Finn said, his head nodding appreciation of the clever device. "I could tell by the way the guy playing Robin Hood stood and held the bow that he'd never hit the target on his own, let alone the centre of it."

"You sound like an expert."

"I guess I am, girl. When I was growing up, down near the Welsh border, we fed our families by our ability with a bow and arrow." He laughed at my incredulous expression. "Yes, we were poachers, but the best meat was the venison on the squire's estate, if we were willing to risk it, and there were always plenty of pheasants and rabbits."

"You could shoot them with an arrow? Seriously?" I was genuinely impressed.

"Oh yes. I can shoot a pheasant out of the air, or I could when I was a young man. I haven't picked one up in a few years and I'm not sure if my eyesight would be good enough now, but I reckon I would have given the real Robin Hood a run for his money."

"Was there a real Robin Hood?" I asked. "I thought he was just a story."

"I don't know, lass. That's a bit before my time. You'd better ask the Reverend." Finn chuckled to himself as he walked across the stage to take another look at the prop's mechanism. "So where do you keep the bow and arrow between shows? Anywhere I can see it?"

"It's under the stage with the rest of the props."

"Can I have a look?"

"Hmm," I thought about it. "I shouldn't really you but you're crew and I know you're not going to do anything dumb, so okay, I'll show you. Just don't tell anyone I let you in."

"My lips are sealed, lass."

"You're lucky I know where the key is kept or I wouldn't be able to show you. And I only know that because my step-dad, Grant, got me to unlock it one day when we got here early for rehearsals. Come on. We have to go down these back stairs."

"How have things been going for you since I last saw you, lass?" Finn asked as we made our way carefully down the steep back stairs to the backstage area.

"Up and down, actually," I admitted. "After the Dilys and Seth thing, I really thought I was changing into one of you, so I've spent the last few months wondering when my fangs and wings would grow. I have to admit it was a huge relief when the Rev explained why that wasn't going to happen."

"You don't fancy becoming one of us?"

"I didn't say that. I'm still thinking about, quite seriously. I just needed a bit longer to get my head around it all. Everything happened in such a rush last time. I just did what needed to be done in the heat of the moment. There wasn't time to make a rational decision. Now there is, so if I do change, it will be because I want to, because it's my choice."

"Severn's a good man," Finn said. "If you did change, he wouldn't let you down. He's loyal. He'd still be standing beside you in a thousand year's time."

"I might have got tired of him by then," I laughed. "I might have swapped him for a five-hundred year old toy boy."

"Or me. You could always swap him for me, lass," Finn said, chuckling at his own joke.

At the foot of the stairs a door led to a room under the stage. By the light of my tiny maglight, I rummaged behind the stairs to find the hidden box that held the key then fumbled with the lock until the door opened. I shone my torch around the small room and spotted the bow and arrow, leant up against the wall in the far corner. Finn picked up the bow, squinting at it in the bad light.

"It's fake," he said. "The woodgrain is just painted on. It's fibreglass."

"Yeah. I don't think they make wooden ones any more. What sort of wood were they? Did they have to be something special?"

"They had to be able to bend without breaking," Finn explained. "Wood from yew trees made good ones, but so did ash and maple. I had a lovely ash one. Used it for years." He strung the bow and flexed it a couple of times. "This isn't great but it's not too bad. It would be adequate for a child to learn on. I don't think it would bring down a deer but that's not what's needed here, is it. Can I take it outside for a better look?"

"It's dark out there." I pointed out.

"But there is a moon and I am a vampire."

I couldn't argue with that so I let Finn take the bow and arrow and followed him out. He was right. The night was much brighter than the total darkness in the small, windowless room. I walked to the side of the stage to see what the others were doing. They were standing together, all staring in the same direction. I looked the same way then ducked back to warn Finn. Meredith and Olivia had arrived.

CHAPTER TWENTY SEVEN

I was going to rush around the stage to join Severn and the others on the lawn but Finn held me back.

"Stay here, lass. Don't get involved. Leave it to Brother Martin and Father David. They know what they are doing. Let's just wait back here and watch, shall we?"

I shrank back into the shadow of the stage and watched the girls striding towards us across the lawn. They were dressed identically in full length, black cloaks, hoods covering their hair, high-heeled, black, leather boots flicking out the bottom as they moved. The men rearranged themselves as the girls approached, Brother Martin and the Reverend moving to the centre of their line, Severn and Aiden taking positions at each end.

The girls stopped halfway across the wide lawn, planting their feet firmly and drawing their cloaks tighter around their bodies.

"Brother Martin, you're an unpleasant surprise," Meredith drawled. "Here we were, coming in good faith for a pleasant business discussion and you boys have brought in the heavy artillery. Such touching faith you have in us, Aiden, my darling twin."

"Hey, don't blame me." Aiden held his hand up in a positon of denial. "I didn't know he was here either until a few minutes ago."

"Of course you didn't. You would never be that treacherous to your sister. But he would," she extended her arm like the Wicked Witch of the West uttering a curse and pointed at Severn. "That little weasel is such a goody two-shoes, with his little human girlfriend and her smarmy little family. I bet he made the call."

She was right but she didn't need to be nasty about it. I wanted to rush over and slap her face but Finn's hand on my shoulder held me in place.

"You've never appreciated the finer and more glorious things about being a vampire, have you, Severn?" Meredith taunted. "Seth knew you hated hunting, that you couldn't bring yourself to hurt anyone. That's why we made you do it. You seem to think it mattered if those ridiculous, expendable, sad drunks lived or died. As if their pathetic, short lives had a purpose."

She paused, waiting for Severn to argue with her but he stood motionless, his feet apart, his arms crossed, his head tilted slightly to the side – the pose I recognised as his silent way of saying "bring it on".

"Oh well, back to you, Brother Martin," Meredith said when the silence lengthened. "You've come to smack our bottoms for being naughty girls, haven't you? But it won't work this time. You're not going to drag us, kicking and screaming, back to that cold, damp, boring hole of a monastery. We are party animals. We need nightlife. Don't you agree, Olivia?"

Meredith looked sideways and Olivia took over with the practised precision of a wrestling tag team.

"We need more than nightlife," Olivia agreed. "We need our own life. Away from you lot. We need big cities with alleyways full of lowlife who won't be missed. We need crowds of humans, their tiny hearts pumping sweet-smelling blood. We don't need meditation and hours of silent prayer."

She stepped forwards one pace. "David, darling, we are going to accept your offer but we want one small change. Berlin instead of Paris. I'm sure you have a lovely house or two there. And we want the deeds to the properties. We want to own them. We don't want to live there, waiting for you to change your mind and kick us out."

"If it gets rid of you, I can agree to that," the Rev agreed. "You are right, Berlin is much better than Paris, so I can do that as long as you agree to stay out of France, out of England and out of New Zealand. Permanently. For ever."

"Oh, that is too easy. We hate all of those boring places," Olivia replied. "Am I hearing you right? Do we have a deal?"

"We have a deal," the Rev confirmed.

"Well, that's peachy. That just leaves one more thing to tidy up," Meredith said. "Aiden, my darling twin brother, come here, my love, so we can say goodbye properly. It may be a very long time before I see you again."

Aiden looked sideways at the others for confirmation then hesitantly walked forwards, his hands outstretched to take the hands Meredith held out to him. Beside me Finn moved, preparing to join his family and farewell his daughter. Olivia was still standing just ahead of Meredith, fingering the toggle on her cloak as she watched Aiden approach. When he reached her, Meredith beamed a smile and took his hands, drawing Aiden close. Olivia pounced.

Before the men had time to react, Meredith had pulled Aiden off balance and snapped a pair of pink, fluffy handcuffs onto his outstretched wrists. Olivia swung her cloak in an arc, wrapping it around Aiden as it fell away from her. Under it, she was in her flight suit – nothing except the shiny, black, knee-high boots.

The men ran towards them but Olivia wrapped her arms around Aiden's chest, spread her wings and flew upwards, effortlessly lifting him into the air. Aiden struggled but, handcuffed and covered by the cloak, he couldn't free himself from her tenacious grip. Even without the cloak, he was still dressed in his blacks and with no way to get his t-shirt off, he would fall before he could unfurl his own wings.

"You're too high. Don't fight her. Keep calm," Severn shouted. "We'll get you."

"No you won't," Meredith said. "If you want him back safe, if you don't want Olivia to drop him, you will do exactly as I say."

"What do you want?"

"You. I want you. I really wanted your little piece of human rubbish. I was expecting her to be locked to your side tonight. It was supposed to be her up there with Olivia and we really were going to drop her. But Aiden's a good substitute. I will feel bad if we have to drop him, I do love my twin, but that's up to you."

"What do I have to do?'

"You have to find your little piece of human trash and give her to me so I can kill her."

Finn pulled me back under the stairs but I didn't need encouragement – I was just glad I hadn't been with Severn when they arrived.

"Why should I do that?" Severn asked. "What have you got against Riley? What did you have against Julia, for that matter? If it's me you're after, I'm right here. Do your worst."

"Julia wanted my man. She needed to pay."

"But your man was already dead. And why Brighton? What the hell is this Brighton beach thing you've been doing for decades? What's that all about?"

"Oh, that was just my little joke with Seth. My anniversary present to him. He turned me on Brighton beach. It's my little bit of nostalgia for times past. Now stop wasting time. Where's your girlfriend? I want her here."

"Why? What's your problem with her that you can't settle with me?"

"I don't have a problem with your girlfriend, except she was there when you ruined my life, and Olivia's life, so it seems like fair payback for us to ruin yours. Tit for tat. An eye for an eye. A girlfriend for a boyfriend. You killed Seth. I kill Riley. Now fetch her!"

"I can't. She's in hospital," Severn lied.

"Then we will hold Aiden until you make the trade. Olivia, darling, take him somewhere safe, where they won't find him."

Above us, Olivia changed from the small wing movements that had been keeping her hovering to stronger beats that lifted her higher. I could see she was beginning to struggle with Aiden's weight as he had slipped down in her grasp. She beat her wings and angled her body to fly sideways, changing her grip on Aiden which left her bare chest now showing white above Aiden's cloak-covered head.

Beside me, Finn had been watching, his gnarled hand clutching my shoulder for reassurance, in fear for his son's life. As Olivia changed position in the air, he gave a small, unintelligible grunt and released his grip. Motioning me to stay still, he stepped away from the stage wall, walked out to where he could see her clearly, and notched the arrow into the bow. Olivia was now over Mona Vale's decorative lake and losing height as her wings tired. Finn took his time. He planted his feet firmly, straightened his back, drew back the bow, and carefully sighted along her line of flight.

"Fly true," he whispered then he held his breath and released the arrow.

It whispered back as it flew towards its target, striking just above Aiden's bowed head. Olivia was flung backwards, losing her grip on Aiden who dropped like a stone into the lake. Olivia's wings flapped in desperation as she dragged at the arrow, trying to pull it from her breast, then her wings drooped and with a plaintive cry, Olivia fell into the water beside him.

Finn dropped the bow and ran towards the lake, beaten there by Brother Martin and the Rev. Meredith watched Olivia fall in disbelief then she, too, ran towards the lake, screaming Olivia's name. While the other three men plunged into the lake to rescue Aiden, Severn walked calmly over to me and kissed me hard. With a tight smile to reassure me, he entered the tiny props room and returned a few seconds later carrying one of the soldier's fake wooden swords.

"This one is for us," he said.

He took my hand and we walked together to the edge of the lake where Aiden sat, wet, gasping but safe. Olivia's body lay on the grass beside him, Meredith crouched at her side, stroking her face and crying. When she saw us, she rose to her knees, hissing a torrent of vile abuse.

"Don't get up," Severn said. "Make this easy." He stepped forwards until he was standing over her, grasped the wooden sword in both hands and lifted it up.

"Back in the theatre, when I drove that pole through your boyfriend, Seth, I should have killed you too. For Finn's sake, for Aiden's sake, I let you live."

He raised his arms and with all his strength, plunged the sword deep into her chest.

"I don't make the same mistake twice."

########

Other Books by J.L. O'Rourke

Blood in the Wings
The First of Severn

Vampires and murder backstage in a Christchurch theatre. 16 year old Riley Lowe is working as a stage hand, backstage at her theatre company's annual show. Her classmate from school, Tasha, is also in the show as a dancer and, as usual, she is flirting with all the guys. In particular, she is trying to take the one Riley is attracted to. Severn is one of a group of professional theatre crew who are helping with the show but the closer she gets to him, the more Riley realises that there is something strange about the group who live and work in the dark. When Tasha is killed and Severn disappears, Riley learns their terrible secret. But can she solve the murder in time to save Severn?

Read an excerpt:

The rain came down red and Severn was gone.

The police asked me lots of questions, both at the theatre and, later, down at the police station but I couldn't tell them much more than that. No, that's not true. I could have told them heaps more, but I didn't. Anyway, I wasn't sure myself. No, don't tell anyone anything. Just answer their questions, get out of here, find Severn and hope the answers are wrong.

"Tell me again, Miss Lowe, take it slowly." The policeman, a detective inspector I think he said he was, kept tapping his pen against the table. It was driving me crazy. The policewoman sitting by the door smiled. That was driving me crazy too.

"What do you know about this Severn?"

I have to think about the answer. I know things about Severn that nobody knows but I hardly know him at all. And I desperately want to keep on learning.

So, really slowly like the cop wants, I start from the beginning again.

"I met Severn two weeks ago when we packed in." It feels like forever.

"Packed in?" the cop inquires.

"Yeah, that's what I said. Pack-in. It's theatre-speak, Get used to it!" This guy was so dumb.

"All right, Miss Lowe," the cop snapped. "There's no need to get abusive. Let's just get on with it so we can all go home."

"Yeah, well don't butt in then!" Okay, it was well after midnight and I was tired and cranky, but he really was a jerk. "I told you, I met him at pack-in. That's when we set up the show in the theatre." I added the last bit slowly, just in case he was as stupid as he looked in his prissy black jacket and his ugly blue tie,

Then, as he still looked blank, I explained.

"Until pack-in the show is all over the place. The actors will have been rehearsing in one place, the orchestra somewhere else and the dancers somewhere else again. The props and the wardrobe have been made at the main rehearsal rooms over the last few months and the sets have been made in a hired warehouse. At least that's how our company usually works."

The cop was rapidly taking notes.

"On pack-in day the set and all the technical stuff such as the lights and the sound gear arrives at the theatre and the crew take over; rigging, wiring, hauling things into place. It's organised chaos. I love it."

"Why were you there?"

"Mum's been in the society for years. Even before she went to Australia and met Dad. When they split up she came home and joined up again. I go with her."

"You act?"

"No, I'm the family disappointment. Backstage, that's my job. I'm doing theatre arts at school but only because it's easy, not because I ever want to act!"

He was actually writing this down, he really was a jerk!

"But you were at this show?" he asked, looking up from his paper.

"Yeah, I just told you, I work backstage. My theatre arts teacher also happened to be the choreographer for this year's show and she talked to the stage manager who agreed I could work as floor crew, moving bits of set on and off stage when the scenes change.

This year's production is the biggest show we've done. The

director decided to have all the scene changes happening with the curtains up but in a black-out and there're about twenty-one scene changes so they needed a lot of crew. That's how come Severn and his lot were there at all. We didn't have enough people to move all the sets by ourselves, or do the complicated lighting the show needs, so the stage manager rang somebody who rang somebody else who suggested Seth Borman.

"Seth Borman," the cop repeated as he wrote the name on his piece of paper.

"That's what I said."

The cop glared at me.

"It was a good idea," I continued. "Even if it is costing the society an arm and a leg. He runs a professional travelling stage crew. Technical wizards."

"And Severn was one of these?" the cop asked.

"Yeah," I snapped back. "I was just getting to that." I carried on.

"Seth Borman's the leader. The head flyman." I could see the cop's eyebrow start to rise with a question so I jumped in first. "Flymen are the guys who work on a little platform about fifteen metres above the stage, hauling the big backdrop cloths and bits of set in and out. They are immensely strong. Seth Borman has an upper body to die for," I added wistfully.

The cop glared at me again. I continued.

"There are six more of them. The women, Olivia and Meredith, work floor crew like I do. So does Aiden, Meredith's twin brother. The older guy, Finn, is the floor electrician. The guy in charge of lighting is a strange little dude they call the Reverend. He's about five foot nothing tall and wears a huge black floor-length coat that makes him look like a miniature version of Darth Vader. I've never seen him without a can of coke in one hand and a chocolate bar in the other.

Severn operates the sound board.

I didn't notice him for the first four days.

Chains of Blood

The Second of Severn.

Riley Lowe is backstage at another show, but this time she

is out of her depth, running equipment she doesn't understand and faced with all sorts of problems including a boy actor who is a spoilt little brat. When her personal vampires arrive to help, Riley thinks everything has suddenly got better, until the boy disappears. Will the vampire's special skills be enough to find the boy and how long will it be before Riley turns into a vampire herself?

Read an excerpt:

I fished a hanky out of my pocket, dried my eyes and blew my nose. Crying was not going to help. But I still had no idea what to do. Maybe Mum and Grant could help. The sound operator from our own theatre company was out of town touring with a fashion show but if Grant could get hold of him, he could at least tell me what to do.

Then my cell phone vibrated in my pocket. I hauled it out and stared at it blankly. A message from a withheld number. Curious, I opened it.

angels r us look up look left

I looked up, peered through the darkness of the encroaching night. Looked left – towards the carpark. And they were there. Three figures emerged out of the gloom, striding side by side like the baddies in a b-grade western or the chorus-line for a musical version of the Matrix, long black coats flowing behind them. Before I could get out of my chair the one in the middle had broken into a run. I have never climbed down the scaffold as quickly, but I was still not at ground level when he reached me, picked me off the scaffold and pulled me into his arms.

When I came up for breath I could see Mum and Grant standing up from where they had been sitting on the grass and walking towards David and Aiden, hands outstretched in welcome.

"What? How? When?" I stuttered, wrapping my arms around Severn's waist under his coat as we walked to join the others.

"Sounded like you needed help," Severn smiled, his arm around my shoulders.

"And we needed sun," Aiden added.

I gave him a quizzical look. "You? Needed sun? Umm...?" The "have you forgotten you're a vampire?" question left unasked.

"Oh no, not in the want-to-hang-out-in-the-daylight way. We were just sick of snow. It is so cold in the mountains."

"And we were bored," the Reverend added. "Sounds like we got here just at the right time. We were in the carpark. We heard the director's little request."

Of course they did. A normal person sitting beside me wouldn't have heard it unless they were wearing headphones but of course the vampires heard it. I wonder how long it takes for things like that to change – my hearing hadn't changed at all yet and it had been three months since I had drunk Severn's blood and started the change-over. I must ask them how long it takes and what the symptoms are.

"How did you get here so quickly? I only emailed you yesterday?"

"We flew," Severn replied with one of his pedantically correct and obvious answers, complete with raised eyebrow over his fine, tortoiseshell-rimmed glasses.

I gave him a similar look back. "Flew? Um, flew... as in...?"

"As in the Lear Jet," Severn laughed. "You weren't thinking...?" and he flexed his shoulders so I could feel his wings move under his t-shirt. "We are not that fast – or that fit."

"Weren't you worried about coming back so soon after ... what if they stopped you at the airport? Don't the police still want to talk to you about the body at New Brighton?"

Power Ride

An Avi Livingstone Murder Mystery

Kester (Kit) Simmons, drummer with the rock band 'Charlotte Jane', was out of beat. He was stressed out, starving and he thought he was going crazy. Then, with less than two weeks to go before a national tour, Kit's precious drums and one of the band members are found slashed to pieces. The keyboard player, Avi Livingstone, is missing, Kit has no alibi and, to make matters worse, the police suspect him of dealing drugs.

Read an excerpt:

"Cousin, tell me something. Kit's a bit out of it, isn't he? Do tours always have this effect on him?"

"Tours? No, they don't affect him at all, strangely enough," Avi replied thoughtfully. "Something is obviously bugging him, though. Mind you, that doesn't mean to say that it'll be anything horrendous. Kit doesn't have the most stable personality and he is apt to make monstrous mountains out of the most minute of molehills. Whatever it is, he doesn't want to talk about it. This, with Kit, means that it is probably something reasonably serious, but I can't force him to talk to me. I'll have another go later. I can usually convince him to talk, it's just a matter of easing him along gently. I can be very persuasive." He ignored Jo's expression of sarcasm. "I wouldn't worry about it too much, though. In the meantime, I would think the best thing we can do is keep Danny from ripping Kit's face off this afternoon."

"Danny doesn't like Kit much, does he?"

"Huh!" Avi's laugh was more a scoff of derision. "Rest assured, cousin dearest, it's nothing personal. This close to a tour, Danny hates everyone, including and especially himself. Tours might not affect Kit, but they blow Danny away. He'll get worse yet."

"Super." Jo did not sound as if she actually meant the superlative. "You mean we're likely to see some fireworks?"

"Better than Old Man Carson's bonfires. I guarantee it."

Joanna laughed and rubbed her hands gleefully. Then she stopped and looked serious.

"But Danny's such a little guy. He wouldn't be stupid enough to upset the whole band would he? Surely?"

"He would, he has and he will, no doubt, do so again. In case you hadn't noticed, Daniel Gordon is somewhat akin to your neighbour's crazed Jack Russell terrier. Wind him up enough and he'll tackle anything, even if it is three times his size. Mind you, we could have some real problems this tour. I don't think it's going to be a very smooth ride. Danny is still very angry about losing our last bass player and, even though we've got Kelly, Danny is determined to hold Kit responsible and to rub it in as much as possible."

"Why?"

Avi shrugged his shoulders and spread his hands wide in a gesture of genuine incomprehension.

"I don't know. Danny's just a creep, I guess."

"So why keep him in the band, if he's such a creep?"

"Two reasons, I guess. He's a damn good guitarist and vocalist and he sells records."

"Garbage! The band sells records, not Danny Gordon. 'Charlotte Jane' was selling records before Danny joined you guys, and who the hell was he? Some two-bit wanna-be from Geraldine! Come on, Avi, he might be a good guitarist but they're ten a penny. If the man is a jerk you've got to have a better reason than that for keeping him on."

Avi ran his hand thoughtfully over his unshaven chin. He shrugged again.

"You know something, Jo? I don't have a decent answer. I guess we've got so used to Danny being a prize prick we just take his temper tantrums for granted. I mean, nobody's perfect, and if we started throwing out band members who had personality problems there'd be bugger all of us left. Poor old Kit would be at the top of the list, he's completely scrambled, and I don't think I'm always the easiest musician to work with. Anyway, whatever Danny is, he's a good businessman. He's got a pretty watertight contract, so we're stuck with him for the duration, at least."

"The duration of what?"

"The cd, the tour and the next single. It could be an exhausting few months."

About the Author

J. L. O'Rourke has worked as a journalist, sub-editor, free-lance writer and office administrator. When not writing, she enjoys being in a theatre, either onstage as a singer or backstage where she has been everything from floor crew to stage-manager. She lives on an olive grove in North Canterbury, New Zealand.

You can follow her on Facebook at
 https://www.facebook.com/MillwheelPress
or on Smashwords,
https://www.smashwords.com/profile/view/millwheel